Escal-Vigor

Escal-Vigor
Georges Eekhoud

MINT EDITIONS

Escal-Vigor was first published in 1899.

This edition published by Mint Editions 2021.

ISBN 9781513295411 | E-ISBN 9781513295565

Published by Mint Editions®

 MINT
EDITIONS
minteditionbooks.com

Publishing Director: Jennifer Newens
Design & Production: Rachel Lopez Metzger
Project Manager: Micaela Clark
Typesetting: Westchester Publishing Services

Contents

PART THE THIRD. THE FAIR OF ST. OLFGAR

PART THE FIRST
THE DYKGRAVE'S RETURN

I

O n the first of June, Henry de Kehlmark, the young "Dykgrave" or
Count of the Dike, the lord of the castle Escal-Vigor, entertained
a numerous company, as a sort of Joyous Entry, to celebrate his home-
coming to the cradle of his forefathers, at Smaragdis, the largest and
richest island in one of those enchanting and heroic northern seas, the
coasts of which the bays and fiords hollow out and cut up capriciously
into multiform archipelagoes and deltas.

Smaragdis, or the Emerald Isle, was a dependency of the half-
German, half-Celtic kingdom of Kerlingalande. At the very beginning
of commercial enterprise in the west, a colony of Hanseatic merchants
settled there. The Kehlmarks claimed descent from the Danish sea-
kings, or Vikings. Bankers, who had in them a dash of pirates' blood,
men both of knowledge and action, they followed Frederick Barbarossa
in his Italian expeditions, and distinguished themselves by an inalterable
devotion, the fidelity of thane to king, to the House of Hohenstaufen.

A Kehlmark had even been the favourite of Frederick II, the Sultan
of Luceria, that voluptuous emperor, the most artistic of the romantic
house of Swabia, who, in that brilliant southern land, lived a life
energised by the deep and virile aspirations of the north. This Kehlmark
perished at Beneventum with Manfred, the son of his illustrious friend.

At the date of our story, a large panel in the billiard room of Escal-
Vigor still represented Conradin, the last of the Hohenstaufens, in the
act of embracing Frederick of Baden before mounting with him on to
the scaffold.

In the Fifteenth century, there flourished at Antwerp a Kehlmark,
money-lender to kings, like the Fuggers and the Salviati, and he figured
among those haughty Hanseatic merchants, whose custom it was to
wend them to the Cathedral, or to the Exchange, preceded by fife and
violin players.

An historic and even legendary abode, suggesting at once a German
castle and an Italian palace, the castle of Escal-Vigor is situated at the
western extremity of the island, at the intersection of two very lofty
dikes, from whence it commands a view of the whole country.

From time immemorial the Kehlmarks had been considered as the
masters and protectors of Smaragdis. The duty of guarding and keeping
in repair the monumental dikes had been their's for centuries. An

ancestor of Henry was credited with the erection of those enormous ramparts, which had for ever preserved the country from those inundations and sometimes total submersions, that had overwhelmed several of the sister-isles.

Once only, about the year 1400, on a wild, tempestuous night, the sea had succeeded in breaking through a part of this chain of artificial hills, and had rolled its cataclysmal waves to the very heart of the island; when, so the tradition runs, the castle of Escal-Vigor proved sufficiently spacious and well-provisioned to serve as refuge and storehouse for the entire population.

The Dykgrave sheltered his people as long as the waters covered the country, and when the flood had abated he not only repaired the dike at his own expense, but also rebuilt the cottages of his vassals. In process of time these dikes, now almost five centuries old, had assumed the appearance of natural hills. On the summit were planted thick curtains of trees, somewhat bent by the west wind. At the highest point the two ranges of hills joined together to form a sort of plateau or promontory, that jutted like a horse-spur, or ship's prow, sheer into the sea, and at the extreme end of this cape the castle stood out like a sentinel. The perpendicular dike presented to the ocean a face of granite wall and recalled those majestic rocks to be found along the Rhine, and out of which the castle crowning the summit looks as if it had been carved.

At high tide, the waves came breaking themselves in baffled rage at the foot of the buttress thrown up to check their fury. On the land side the two dikes sloped gently away, and, as they separated, their branches formed a small valley, which gradually grew larger, enclosing a magnificent park, with forests, pond and pastures. The trees, that were never pruned, spread out their wild foliage like immense fans, ever quivering in the wind like the sound of Aeolian harps. Herds of wild deer passed in their flight, like yellow flashes of lightning, amid the dense vegetation; while cows browsed on that moist and succulent herb, of an almost fluid green tint, to which the island owes its name of Emerald.

Notwithstanding the popularity of the Kehlmarks in the district, the castle had for the last twenty years remained uninhabited. The mutual affection of the young and handsome parents of the present Count had been so intense that the one could not survive the other. Henry was born there some months before their death. His paternal grandmother, who took charge of him, refused ever to set foot again in the country, to the ravages of whose inclement climate she attributed the premature death of her children. Henry, accordingly, was brought up on the continent, in the capital of the kingdom of Kerlingalande; and afterwards by the advice of physicians, he was sent to study at an international boarding-school in Switzerland.

There, at Bodemberg Castle where he passed his youth, he long wore the look of a fair, rather delicate adolescent, cursed with a tendency to anaemia and consumption; he had a reflective, somewhat intense expression of countenance, a broad, roundish forehead, cheeks the colour of a rose on the fade, whilst a precocious fire burnt in a pair of large, dark-blue coloured eyes, akin to the violet of amethyst, or the purple of the clouds and waves at sunset. His head, somewhat too massive, seemed with its weight to crush his sloping shoulders; his limbs were feeble, and his chest devoid of firmness. The weakly constitution of the little Dykgrave would have exposed him to the rough horseplay of his fellow-pupils had he not escaped this by the prestige of his intelligence, a prestige that had its effect even on the professors. All respected his need of solitude and reverie, his propensity to avoid the customary amusements, his liking to walk alone in the depths of the park, with no companion save a favourite author, or, more frequently, contenting himself with the society of his own thoughts. His ill-health still further increased his susceptibility. Headaches and intermittent fevers kept him often a-bed, isolating him for several days at a stretch.

Once, just after he had attained his fifteenth year, he was almost drowned, in an excursion on the water, a school-fellow with him having upset the boat. For several weeks he lay between life and death. Then, by a strange caprice of nature, it fell out that the very accident which had almost carried him off, brought about a salutary crisis, and produced that reaction so long desired by his grandmother, who looked upon him as her last hope and stay on earth. In agreement with the young Count's guardians, she had selected this distant school, because it Was at once a model college and a fine health residence, in the most salubrious part of Switzerland. Before being converted into a cosmopolitan academy—it was intended for young patricians of both hemispheres—Bodemberg-Schloss had been a fashionable bathing establishment, the resort of the most elegant invalids of Switzerland and Germany. Henry's grandmother had therefore naturally counted upon the healthy climate of the Aar valley, and the hygienic advantages of this educational establishment, more closely to bind to life and possibly to effect the complete regeneration of this the sole descendant of an illustrious race. For was not this idolised grandson of hers the only offspring left by her departed children, whom excess of love had early slain?

Kehlmark not only recovered his health, but found himself in possession of quite a new constitution. Not only did a rapid convalescence restore to him his former strength but, to his surprise, he saw himself growing taller, walking with a more elastic step, getting a bigger chest and harder muscles and gaining in flesh and fulness of blood. With this rejuvenescence of the body there came to Kehlmark a frankness and ingenuousness of the soul, of the warmth and tenderness of which, his over-studious and reflective mind had until then been wholly unaware.

Although he had formerly looked with contempt upon athletic exercises, he now applied himself to vigorous training, and in the end came to be quite an athlete. Far from shrinking, as before, from the risk of violent exertion, he distinguished himself by his boldness and enthusiasm. He, who in order to save himself the fatigue of a climb in the Jura, had often hidden away in the subterraneous passages, amongst the heating apparatus of the ancient bathing establishment, was now conspicuous among the most indefatigable of mountain climbers.

At the same time he remained a reader and a student, being at once a great amateur of deeds of physical prowess and of sporting games of skill, recalling in this respect the accomplished men and harmonious livers of the Renaissance.

On the death of his grandmother whom he adored, he had come back and taken up residence in his native country, a filial affection for which had clung to him from boyhood, and whose impulsive and outspoken denizens would naturally be pleasing to his frank and generous mind.

The aborigines of Smaragdis belonged to that Celtic race, from which the Bretons and the Irish have sprung. In the Sixteenth century inter-marriage with the Spaniards intensified and perpetuated the predominance of dark blood over the blond. Kehlmark knew that these islanders, who, with their swarthy and strongly-marked complexions, were very distinct from the pink-and-white skinned peoples that surrounded them, had made themselves exceptional also by the stubborn resistance they had offered to the introduction of Christian, and especially of Protestant, morals. At the time of the conversion of these countries, the barbarians of Smaragdis submitted to baptism, only as the result of a war of extermination which the Christians waged against them to avenge the death of the apostle St. Olfgar, whose martyrdom, with an accompaniment of all sorts of cannabalistic inventions, is scrupulously, and as it were professionally, depicted in frescoes adorning the parish church of Zoutbertinge, the work of a pupil of Thierry Bouts, pourtrayer of men flayed alive. The legend runs that the women of Smaragdis had particularly distinguished themselves in this butchery. They had even added outrageous indecency to ferocity, having wrought with Olfgar even as the Bacchantes had with Orpheus.

Oft-times, in the course of the ages, heresies of sensual and subversive nature had arisen in this country of fiery temperraments and unconquerable independence. In the kingdom of Kerlingalande, now become very Protestant, where strict Lutheranism reigned as the State religion, the deep-sunken and occasionally explosive impiety of the population of Smaragdis was one of the chief cares of the Consistory.

Accordingly, the bishop of the diocese, on which the island was dependent, had lately sent a militant pastor, a man right full of craft, a sectary unhealthy and bilious, named Balthus Bomberg, who was burning to distinguish himself, and who came to Smaragdis somewhat in the spirit of a crusader against a new set of Albigenses.

His christianising efforts were, without doubt, pre-destined to prove quite useless. In spite of orthodox pressure, the island preserved its original fund of licence and paganism. The heresies of the Antwerp men Tanchelin and Pierre l'Ardoisier, that five centuries earlier had agitated the neighbouring countries of Flanders and Brabant, had struck their roots deep down into Smaragdian soil and strengthened the primitive character of the people.

All sorts of traditions and customs, abhorred in the other provinces, continued here notwithstanding ecclesiastical anathemas and priestly admonitions. The annual Fair used to prove the occasion for the outbreaking of sensual riots more savage and unbridled than in Friesland, or in Zealand, well renowned for the frenzy of their festivals; and every year at this epoch it seemed that the women were dominated by much of that same sanguinary hysteria that had erstwhile inflamed the tormentresses of good Bishop Olfgar.

By that strange law of contrasts, in virtue of which extremes meet, these islanders, though devoid of any definite religion, remained superstitious and fanatical, like the natives of most countries subject to phantasmal mists and fallacious meteors. Their love of the marvellous descended to them from remote theogonies, the gloomy and fatalistic cults of Thor and Odin; but eager appetites were mingled with their fantastic imaginations, intensifying their affections as well as their aversions.

II

Henry, whose nature was passionate and philosophy audacious, told himself, not without reason, that through his affinities, he would feel himself at home amid these beautifully barbarous surroundings, where natural instincts reigned.

He even inaugurated his accession as "Dykgrave," with an innovation, against which the minister Balthus Bomberg was infallibly bound to fulminate from the full height of his pastoral desk. To flatter the native sentiment, Henry had invited to his table not only a few squires and landed proprietors, and a few artists from among his town friends, but he had also summoned around him a crowd of simple farmers, small ship-owners, masters of sailing-vessels and barges of the lowest class, the lighthouse-keeper, the lock-keeper, the heads of the dikemen's gang, and even simple labourers. These natives he had further invited to bring to his house-warming their wives and daughters.

All the guests, both men and women, had dressed themselves at his particular request, either in the national costume, or in their personal uniform. The men arrayed themselves in velvet vests of a reddish-brown colour, or of a blinding red, worn over embroidered flannels on which were represented the instruments of their profession, anchors, ploughing implements, bulls' heads, navigators' instruments, sunflowers, sea-gulls, the almost oriental medley of colours standing out with peculiar effect on the sea-blue ground, like armorial bearings on a shield. On their broad, red belts shone old silver buckles of a workmanship at once barbarous and touching; others exhibited the sculptured oaken handles of their broad clasp-knives; the sea folk paraded in great tarred boots; delicate metal rings adorned the lobe of their ears, which were as red as shellfish: the farm labourers wore trousers of the same velvet as their vests, and these trousers, tight above, enlarged from the calf to the instep after the style known as "bell-bottoms." Their small hat recalled that of the lawyers' clerks of the time of Louis XI. The women displayed head-dresses of lace topped by conical hats with broad strings; their bodices being more variegated, and ornamented with interlacings even more capricious than the men's waistcoats; they wore bulging petticoats of the same velvet and the same reddish-brown shade as the vests and the breeches; thin gold chains were three times wound around their throats and in their ears were ear-drops of an ancient, quasi-byzantine pattern, whilst on their fingers they sported rings with bezels as thick as those of a bishop.

These folk were, for the most part, robust specimens of the dark-complexioned type of that ardent and full-blooded race of swarthy, sinewy Celts, with rebellious, woolly locks. Bronzed peasants and sailors, a little embarrassed at the beginning of the repast, they had soon recovered their assurance. With clumsy gestures, but by no means artificial, and often even, after a manner newly discovered by themselves, deftly they plied knife and fork. As the meal progressed, tongues loosened, and bursts of laughter sometimes interspersed with an oath, seasoned their guttural speech, which, although highly coloured revealed smooth unexpected notes of caressing tenderness.

Logical in his disregard of etiquette and in violation of all rules of precedence, the host had had the happy thought, in each case, to seat a farmer's wife, the mistress of a boat, or a fish-wife, by the side of one of his peers of the oligarchy; and similarly, beside some proud lady from a neighbouring château was wedged in a young dairyman of swaggering manner, or a boatman boasting knotty biceps.

Kehlmark's friends remarked that almost all the guests were in the flower of their youth, or in the first flush of their maturity. One might have called the gathering a selection of prepossessing women and of malleable, impressionable youths.

Among the guests was to be found one of the principal agriculturists of the country, Michel Govaertz, of the farm "Les Pelerins." He was a widower and the father of two children, Guidon and Claudie.

After the lord of Escal-Vigor, the farmer of Les Pelerins was the most important man of Zoudbertinge village, on the territory of which was situated the country-seat of the Keklmarks.

During the minority and in the absence of the young Count, Govaertz had replaced him at the head of the Wateringue, or committee for the maintenance and preservation of the alluvial lands, called "polders," of which committee the Dykgrave was the leading member. And it was not without some certain mortification to his self-esteem, that, on the return of Kehlmark, the farmer of Les Pelerins had seen himself reduced to the rank of a simple member of the assemblies in question. But the young Count's affability had soon made Govaertz forget this slight decrease of his authority. Then, he sat before in the Wateringue only as representative of the Dykgrave, while as juryman he had the right of initiative and of voting in the chapter. Moreover, had he not been recently elected burgomaster of the parish?

A stout peasant, a man of forty and of goodly presence, not ill-natured, but very conceited, and without character, he had felt extremely flattered at being invited to the château to occupy with his daughter the head of the table. Supported by his cronies, above all egged on and put up to it by his daughter, the not less ambitious but more intelligent Claudie, he incarnated the privileges and civil liberties of the community, setting rebelliously pastor Bomberg at defiance. For a moment, he feared lest the Count of Kehlmark should use his influence to get himself appointed magistrate of the village. But Henry detested politics, with the jealousies they engender, the acts of baseness, the intrigues, the compromises they impose upon public men. On this side therefore, Govaertz had nothing to fear. He accordingly, resolved to make a friend and ally of the great lord, in order to reduce the minister to impotence. This policy, as soon as the arrival of the owner of Escal-Vigor was known, had been recommended to him by Claudie.

For the greater honouring of the Burgomaster, the Count had seated Claudie Govaertz on his right.

Claudie, the strong mind of the family, was a tall, full-bodied girl, with the temperament of an amazon, voluminous breasts, muscular arms, robust but elastic figure, hips like a young cow's; and a commanding voice, a type of the virago and the valkyrie. An abundant chignon of golden-brown hair helmeted her wilful head, and spread its locks over a low forehead, reaching well-nigh down as far as her bold, impudent eyes, that were brown and liquid as molten bronze, the coarse challenge in them being emphasised by a wide straight nose, a greedy mouth, and carnivorous teeth. A thing compact of flesh and instincts was she, craving for power, a fierce ambition alone being able to keep her appetites in check, and preserving her up to the present chaste and inviolate, in spite of her nature's passionate warmth. Not a shadow of feeling or of delicacy. A will of iron and no scruple in reaching her ends. Since the death of her mother, that is to say, since her seventeenth year—she was now twenty-two—she had ruled the farm, the household, and up to a certain point, the parish. It was with her that the pastor had to reckon. Her brother Guidon, a youth of eighteen years, and even her father the burgomaster, trembled when she raised her voice. Being one of the best matches of the island, she had not been a little sought after, but had refused even the wealthiest suitors, for did she not dream of a marriage which should raise her above all the other women of the country? This was the reason even of her virtue. A splendid and vibrating piece of flesh, attracted herself as much as she allured, she discouraged the serious attentions of males on matrimony bent, although, God wot, willingly would she have abandoned herself to them, swooned away in their arms and returned readily enough embrace for embrace; or, who can tell, perhaps, provoked caresses, and had needs been, have taken them by force.

The better to deaden and stifle her desires, Claudie spent her strength during the week in drudgery, in fatiguing labours, and at the periodical fairs gave herself up to furious dancing, teased men to horseplay, exciting amongst her gallants riots and quarrels; and then, deceiving the victor's hopes, overpowering him if necessary, affecting a roughness greater even than his, going indeed so far as to strike him and to treat him as he had treated his rivals, she would slip off untouched. Or, if it happened that she did slyly return a caress or tolerated some anodyne familiarity, she kept cool enough to recollect herself at the critical moment, recalled to modesty by her dream of a glorious establishment.

As soon as she had set eyes upon Henry de Kehlmark, she vowed in her heart to become mistress of Escal-Vigor.

Henry was a handsome cavalier, a bachelor, fabulously rich the report went, and as well-born as the King. Cost what it might he should marry this haughty female. Nothing easier than to make herself beloved by him. Had she not turned the heads of all the young villagers? The proudest would have yielded to any terms in order to win her. She would like, forsooth, to see if a man would refuse her, when once she was only willing to surrender herself to him!

Claudie already knew, through having caught sight of her in the park or on the shore, that the Count was accompanied by a young woman, his housekeeper, or rather his mistress. This illicit connection indeed had put the finishing touch to minister. Bomberg's holy wrath. But Claudie was not overmuch disturbed by the presence of this person. Kehlmark did not seem to make much of her. As a proof, the young lady had not even appeared at table. Claudie flattered herself she could get her dismissed and, if necessary, replace her until the marriage should take place; for she was confident enough of her power, to give herself up to Kehlmark and compel him afterwards to marry her. Besides, our Jordaenesque female looked upon as only very insignificant that pale, weak, little, woman, whose person, lean and suggestive of anaemia, was devoid of all those robust corporal attractions that rustics prize so highly.

No, the Count of the Dike would not long hesitate between that mincing-mannered young lady and the superb Claudie, the most dazzling female in Smaragdis, aye, the most dazzling in all Kerlingalande.

During the dinner, she took the measure of the man, with the wanton looks and perspicacity of a Bacchante, while she estimated the furniture and the plate at the same time with the eye of an auctioneer, or of a village notary. The value of the estate had long been known to her, as to everybody else in the village. This large triangular vale, bounded on two sides by dikes, and on the third by an iron gate and wide ditches, represented, with the dependent farms and woods, almost a tenth of the entire island. And further, public rumour ascribed to Kehlmark possessions in Germany, in the Netherlands, and in Italy.

It was also reported that his grandmother, the dowager, had left him nearly three millions of florins invested in the funds. No more was necessary for Claudie to consider Kehlmark highly eligible as a husband. Perhaps, if he had not been rich and titled, she would have preferred him somewhat more stout-limbed and full-blooded. But she never tired of admiring his elegance, his aristocratic features, his ladylike hands, his fine ultramarine eyes, his silken moustache, and his carefully trimmed beard. Even what the Dykgrave sometimes showed of reserve or timidity in his character, of languor or melancholy, was by no means displeasing to the gross-minded woman. Not that she was subject to sentimentalism: nothing, on the contrary, was further from her extremely coarse character; but because Kehlmark's moments of reverie seemed to her to betray a weak nature, a passive disposition, she would rule all the more easily over his person and his property.

Yes, this noble personage should prove malleable and ductile to the last degree. How, otherwise, would he have submitted so long to the yoke of that makeshift of a "miss," whom the over-expeditious Claudie was already not far from regarding as an intruder? The reasoning which the sturdy wench indulged in was not entirely devoid of logic: "If he has allowed himself to be ensnared and dominated by that impertinent minx, how much more quickly would he be subjugated by a proper sort of woman?"

Henry's manners were not adapted to undeceive her. He displayed a feverish gaiety the whole of the time, the gaiety almost of a man too deeply preoccupied with his thoughts and seeking distraction;

he tormented and excited his fair neighbour at the table with such persistence that she believed she had already attained her ends. This recklessness on Kehlmark's part went so far as to scandalise the few squires invited to these eccentric "love-feasts," but they concealed their feelings, and although laughing inwardly at this ridiculous gathering, which they had consented to attend only out of regard for the rank and fortune of the Dykgrave, they affected, in his presence, to consider the idea of this house-warming as supremely aesthetic, and loudly expressed their admiration. We leave it to be guessed in what terms they told the story of this unseemly masquerade to the minister and his wife, whose flock was made up of these over-grave and ultra-pedantic noblings together with a few bigoted ladies. One after the other they had their carriages called and slipped quietly away with their prudish wives and daughters. The company but enjoyed themselves all the better for their departure.

The Count, who drew and painted like a professional artist, amused himself over the coffee by making a rather smart and pretty sketch of Claudie, which he offered to her, after it had been passed round for the astonishment of the natives, who were more and more delighted with the frank manners of their young Dykgrave. Michel Govaertz, was particularly raised to the seventh heaven flattered by the Count's attentions to his favourite child. Each time Henry had raised his glass to hers, when drinking, nor did he cease to compliment her on her costume: "It becomes you admirably!" said he. "How much more natural you appear in such garments than that lady down there, who gets herself decked out at Paris!"

And, with a look, he pointed out a baroness dolly-vardened up and lavishly dressed out to the nines, seated at the other end of the table, and who, flanked by a couple of free-and-easy going sailors, had maintained, ever since the soup had been served, a disgusted pout and a haughty silence.

"Fie!" Claudie had replied, "you're not in earnest, Monsieur le Comte. It is well that you prescribed to us the costume of the country, otherwise I should have dressed myself up as much as our ladies of Upperzyde."

"I implore you," replied the Count, "beware of such tasteless finery; it would be committing an act of treason!"

And thereupon, he launched out into a panegyric of the national costumes, naively adapted to the particular circumstances of the country, according to differences of nationality and race.

"Dress," he declared, "completes the human type. Let us have our special style of clothing just as we have our special flora and fauna!" his picturesque words seeming to paint and pourtray beautiful human forms harmoniously draped.

At the height of his ethological lecture he perceived that the young peasant girl was indeed listening, but without at all understanding the meaning of his enthusiasm.

In order to divert her, he took upon himself to show her the various apartments of the newly restored château, chock-full of souvenirs and relics. Claudie took the Count's arm, and leading the way, he invited the other villagers to follow, file after file. Claudie's eyes, like two burning coals, devoured the gold of the frames, of the panellings, and of the candelabra, the feudal tapestries, the panoplies of rare arms, but remained unmoved by the art, the taste, the fine ordonnance of these luxurious accessories. Nude nobles, painted or sculptured, among others copies of the young men of Buonarotti surrounding, as with a frame the celebrated compositions on the ceiling of the Sixtine chapel, only struck her on account of their absolute nakedness. Throwing her head backwards she would burst out into a bold, vulgar laugh, or else, covering her face, she pretended to be shocked, whilst her bosom meanwhile rose and swelled; and Kehlmark could feel her trembling and panting against his hips. Michael Govaertz followed in their steps with the lively but bewildered band of villagers. Some of the ignorant clowns made comments on the canvasses of masters, smacking their jaws at one another and, in front of the mythological nudities, indicated their choice with a wink of the eye and even other significant gestures.

Several times the Burgomaster turned round and recommended them to adopt more seemly behaviour.

As he returned from his vain endeavour to recall them to decency, he said: "Someone who is not pleased to see you among us, Count, is our minister, Dom Balthus Bomberg."

"Oh really now!" replied the Dykgrave. "How can I possibly offend him? I do not attend church, it is true, but I believe I know as much about the question of religion as he does, and as for real genuine virtue, I get along well with good men of all creeds. That reminds me, Dom Balthus declined my invitation today, giving me to understand that such promiscuous meetings were repugnant to his character. There's evangelicalism for you! He's a nice man to his parishioners! Isn't he?"

"Do you know he has already preached against you?" said Claudie.
"Indeed? he does me too much honour."

"He did not attack you directly and took care not to name you," the
Burgomaster continued, "but all those present understood that he
referred to your lordship, when he denounced "those fine gentlemen
come from the capital, who proclaim infidel opinions, and who, wanting
in all their duties, set a bad example to poor parishioners, in making
light, with their dissolute manners, of the holy sacrament of marriage!"
And so on and so forth! It appears he gave them a good quarter of an
hour of it, at least, according to what my devotees of sisters tell us, for
neither I nor mine set foot in his church!"

On hearing this allusion to his irregular establishment, the Count
had slightly changed colour, and his nostrils even showed a nervous
contraction of anger, which did not escape Claudie.

"Shall we not have the honour of paying our respects to Madame—
or, shall I rather say, Mademoiselle. . . ?" inquired the peasant girl, with
affected hesitation.

A further expression of suppressed discontent passed over Kehlmark's
countenance. Nor did the passing cloud escape the notice of the crafty
village wench. "So much the better," she mused, "the pretentious hussy
seems to pall upon him already."

"You mean Mademoiselle Blandine, my housekeeper," said Kehlmark
with a gay air!

"Excuse her. She is very busy, and besides, extremely timid. Her great
pleasure consists in preparing and managing behind the scenes my little
receptions. She is in a way my master of the ceremonies, the general
steward of Escal-Vigor."

He laughed, but Claudie seemed to detect in his laugh something
pinched and throttled. On the other hand, it was with a truly softened
intonation that he added: "She is almost a sister. She was present with
me when my grandmother 'closed her eyes for the last time'."

After a short silence: "And you will come to see us at 'Les Pelerins',
Count," asked Claudie, a little disturbed in her matrimonial speculations
by the almost fervent tone of Kehlmark's last words.

"Yes, Count, you would do us great honour by such a visit," added
the Burgomaster: "Without boasting, "Les Pelerins" has not its equal in
the whole kingdom. We have none but cattle of the choicest kind, prize
specimens, the cows and horses no less than the pigs and sheep."

"Rely on me," said the young man.

"Doubtless Monsieur le Comte knows the whole country?" inquired Claudie.

"Well, yes, nearly so. The aspect is very varied. Upperzyde has left in my mind the recollection of a pretty little town, with monuments and even a curious museum. I discovered there once a very agreeable Frans Hals: Ah, a chubby-faced boy, a player on the pipe; the most wonderful symphony of flesh, decoration, and atmosphere, with which this productive and virile artist has ever enchanted the canvas. For this charming little rascal I would give all the Venuses, even those of Rubens,—I must return to Upperzyde."

He stopped short, remembering that to these good people he was only talking Greek.

"I have been informed," he resumed, "of the dunes and heaths at Klaarvatsch. Wait now! Are there not there some very bizarre parishioners?"

"Ah, the savages!" exclaimed the Burgomaster, with an air of protection and contempt. "A population of noisy braggarts! The only vagabonds and mendicants of the country! Our Guidon, my ne'er-do-well of a son, has'gone amongst them! Sad to say, he might be one of them!"

"I will ask your son to guide me there one day, Burgomaster," said Kehlmark, leading his guests into another apartment. His eyes had brightened at the recollection of the little pipe-player. Now they were veiled, and his voice had in it a trembling, an accent of indescribable melancholy, followed by a sort of sob disguised as a cough. Claudie kept looking right and left, casting up the market value of the various knick-knacks and curiosities that fell under her notice.

In the billiard room, which they had just entered, an entire wall was covered, as is well known, by *Conradin and Frederick of Baden*, a painting done by Kehlmark himself from an engraving very popular in Germany. The last kiss of the two young princes, victims of Charles of Anjou, gave their faces an expression of deep, almost sacramental, love, which had been rendered with great intensity by Henry.

—"That? . . . Two young princes. The masters of one of my distant ancestors. They are about to be beheaded," he explained in a strange tone of raillery, to Claudie, who yawned before this painting almost like a lounger used to public executions.

"Poor children!" remarked the robustious girl. "They embrace each other like lovers."

"They loved each other well!" murmured Kehlmark, as though he were saying *Amen!* whilst he drew his companion away. As she naively called attention to the abundance of statues and of nude male figures among the pictures and marbles, he said, "Why yes, they are really the sort of things such as are to be found at Upperzyde and in other museums, you know! They serve after all to fill up the place! For lack of models I use them as copies." Kehlmark spoke these words with an indifferent tone, mimicking, one might well have suspected, the ignorant chatter of the uneducated folk he was piloting.

Was he laughing in his sleeve at his guests or, rather keeping watch and ward over himself?

In accordance with the custom of the village they had sat down to table at noon. It was now nine o'clock and the hour of nightfall.

All at once there was heard a banging and snorting of musical instruments.

Torches drew nigh out of the darkness keeping step with the cadenced measure of open-air serenades, and their curious gleam shed into the half-shadow of the large apartments a strange reddishness like the uncertain light of an aurora borealis.

III

"What's this? treason, an ambush!" exclaimed Kehlmark, assuming a puzzled air. "Our young people of the guild of St. Cecile, our Harmonic Society, who come to bid you welcome, Count," the farmer of Les Pelerins explained with ceremony.

Kehlmark's eyes flashed furtively:

"Another time, I will show you my studio. Let us go and receive them," he said, turning back and hastening down the grand staircase, happy enough, it seemed, at this diversion, which caused the crafty Claudie however to fret inwardly.

The Govaertzes and the others followed him downstairs into the extensive orange-house, the large glass doors of which had been opened by order of the still invisible Blandine.

The musicians of the guild had drawn themselves up in a half-circle at the foot of the flight of steps. They blew with all the force of their lungs into the wide-bellied trumpets, and hammered away conscientiously at the asses' skin of their drums.

All wore, with some differences, the picturesque costume of the youth of the country. With many, their toggery over-worn and even patched, contracted more verdigris and stew than the over-new clothes of the guests. There were some whose dress was in frank disorder; they were without vest, in shirt sleeves, and, with their blouse wide-open, displayed their huge necks as low down as the origin of the pectoral muscles.

They were, almost all of them, tall, sturdy boys, fine strapping dark fellows, recruited from all the castes of the island, from the farms of Zoudbertinge as well as the kennels of Klaarvatsch. The guild, being of a very democratic nature, mingled the sons of the most respectable citizens with the male offspring of plunderers of wrecks and shore vagabonds.

The youngest of these grandsons of wreckers, urchins with rough-tossed hair, wild but brilliant eyes, faces brown as those of Guido's angels, and stout-limbed already, with their breeches held up by rope in place of braces, and ending at the knees in a band adorned with thorns and dead leaves, filled the office of torch-bearers, for a tip of a few coppers. And under pretence of reviving the brightness of their light, but in reality for amusement, they would, every now and then, turn their lanterns upside down, and bespatter the ground with burning tongues of resin, to extinguish which they would then trample under foot, without fear of burning their bare soles that had become as hard as iron.

In honour of the Dykgrave, the St. Cecile guild played very old native tunes, which harmonised in an indescribable manner with the perfumed warmth of the evening. One of them especially, saddened Henry and astonished him in a delightful manner by a melody, plaintive as the ebb-tide, as the gust of wind on the heather, and the imitative sing-saws that the dikemen chaunt when driving piles in the river bed. These workingmen, or rather the heads of gangs, sing these monotonous refrains to put heart into their men as they toil. Each man harnessed to a rope, they simultaneously raise in the air the heavy ram, and then let it fall again. Their legs bend, their bodies stoop, and their haunches regain the upward position in cadence. The same air is to be heard on board fishing-sloops. Sea-faring men take their instrument with them, and with rhapsodies and bucolic songs, beguile the often wearisome hours and the flat calms of the open sea, adapting their plaintive and languishing refrain to the panting rhythm of the waves.

One of the youths, a pupil of the music school at Upperzyde, had transcribed this song for the fanfare. The little bugle-player shrilled out this somewhat hoarse melody to an accompaniment of trumpets and trombones, recalling the deep bass of the rolling surge.

Kehlmark noted the bugle-player, a youth taller and better formed than his companions of his own age. He had rounded hips, an amber-like complexion, eyes of velvet under long black lashes, red, fleshy lips, nostrils dilated as by some mysterious sensual olfactiveness and thick black hair. His wretched costume fitted him well, adhering to his limbs like fur to the elastic body of a cat. His body, with its graceful twisting and balancing, seemed to follow the sound-waves of the music, and he performed on the spot a very slow dance, comparable to the trembling of aspens on those summer nights, when the breeze is reduced to a gentle zephyr that only plants may breathe. The sculptural contour of this young rustic, who united the muscular relief of his compeers to a certain correctness of outline, recalled exactly to Kehlmark the *Pipe player* of Frans Hals. This youth seemed to him a wonderful living picture of the canvas in the Upperzyde museum. His heart tightened; he held his breath, a prey to overpowering emotion.

Michel Govaertz, having noticed the attention which the Dykgrave bestowed on the young soloist, seized the opportunity of the pause which followed, to accost the latter and led him by the ear, so roughly as to risk bruising it, towards Kehlmark.

Nothing could justly render the expression, at once piteous, scared, and rapt, of the young bugle-player, when thus suddenly confronted with the Dykgrave. It seemed as though in his eyes and on his lips was concentrated all the sublime distress of a martyr.

"Count," exclaimed the coarse-grained man, sneeringly, "this is my son Guidon, the scapegrace of whom I spoke to you just now." Making the youth turn round, he continued, "This is the companion of the rascals of Klaarvatsch, a hopeless idler, a good-for-nothing, who combines perhaps all the throat-qualities of finches and larks, but who possesses none of those merits which I looked for in a boy of my blood. Ah! day-dreaming, whistling, cooing in the void, gaping at gulls, lying at full length on his back or basking in the sun like seals on a sand bank, that is what suits him! Just imagine, since his birth he has never been of use to us. As he did not help us at all on the farm I thought of making a sailor of him, and I got him enrolled as cabin boy on a fishing smack. In vain! After three days a boat returning to the port brought him back. In the midst of the tacking he would stop short to look at the clouds and the waves. His heedlessness and negligence cost him some severe drubbings, but blows no more got the better of him than remonstrances and exhortations. Weary of the struggle, I was obliged to take him back and put him to half-a-wake work. Now he looks after the cows and sheep on the moors of Klaarvatsch, with those lousy little beggars who are bearing this evening the torches for the Guild. Well-built as you see him, Sir, is it not a shame P And with all that a cry-baby! He begins to bray, feels ill, when a pig is killed at the fair, or when the butcher marks with red chalk the backs of those sheep that are to be converted into mutton! Guidon is a girl spoiled. My real boy is our Claudie. Ah! she's the sort of girl to get through work for you!"

"It is a pity; he has in spite of that a very intelligent air," remarked the Dykgrave, with as much indifference as possible. "And he plays the bugle admirably too! Why don't you make him seriously a musician?"

"Oh, yes! Now, you're joking, Count. He is incapable of sticking to anything profitable. Upon my honour, so as to get rid of him, I have already tried to hand him over to the mountebanks. Perhaps he'd have made a good buffoon. Meanwhile, he's nothing but a source of damage and slights to me. Thus, he has taken it into his head to scrawl over with charcoal the newly whitewashed walls of the farm under pretext of drawing our cattle!"

"Would he then have any talent for painting?" suggested Kehlmark, with a bored air, affecting even to suppress a yawn.

Guidon's comrades made a circle around the Govaertzes and Kehlmark, amusing themselves with the confusion of the little shepherd-lad, thus placed by his own father on the stool of repentance. The scamps fluttered about, and gave each other elbow digs in the ribs, emphasising, with laughter and murmurs, the complaints which the Burgomaster made about his son.

Together with Guidon, Henry felt himself the object of all this bantering. Claudie regarded her brother with harsh and malevolent looks. Henry guessed that the Burgomaster disparaged and decried his boy thus in order to flatter Claudie, his favourite. Between this rough, mannish girl and the almost refined young peasant, the incompatibility was bound to be extremely irritating. It occurred to Henry that there must be violent quarrels at the fireside of the Govaertzes, and he felt a singular tightness of heart at the thought. Claudie, too, seemed to him visibly provoked by the attention shown by the Dykgrave to this child who was repudiated, put under the ban, and living almost on the outskirts of the family.

"Listen, Burgomaster, we'll talk about it again some other time!" Kehlmark resumed. "It may be possible after all to make something of your wayward boy."

Words, non-committal enough, and pledging him to nothing, but, in speaking them, Henry could scarcely refrain from turning his eyes an instant towards the shepherd-lad, and in this look the latter read, or at least thought he read, a promise something more serious than was contained in the words themselves. The poor youngster felt joy full of hope and of comforting augury. No one had ever looked at him in such a way, or rather, he had never seen so much kindness in a face. But perhaps, the troublesome youth only deceived himself! The Count would have indeed been foolish to take an interest in a fellow so badly recommended by the farmer of "Les Pelerins." Who would think of embarrassing himself with such savage stock, a weed of such ill-growth?

"If only Claudie doesn't tell him too much ill of me!" mused the little shepherd fellow, alarmed at seeing the Dykgrave carried off and taken aside by the terrible sister. But Kehlmark withdrew in order to give orders to Blandine. The musicians were supplied with drink. When the Count returned to toast their healths, how did it happen that he omitted to chink his glass against that held out to him—Oh so devotedly!—by the Burgomaster's son? The latter experienced a moment of sadness, but recollected immediately the tender look of a few moments before. He left the drinkers, to wander through the rooms and, in his turn, admire the pictures. Although ostensibly engaged in paying court to the buxom Claudie, Henry more than once glanced furtively at the young bugle-player of the Guild. He caught the youth's expression, at once reflective and ecstatic, before *Conradin and Frederick*, which his sister had just looked at with the interest only of a reader of police-court cases, or celebrated torture-scenes.

With glasses of full measure the Dykgrave had done honour to the rough serenaders. He even seemed to them a trifle tipsy, but this was a matter not at all likely to shock them, for the natives of Smaragdis were deep drinkers like most men of the north.

The company, happy to disport themselves, spread out over the gardens and along the shore, which soon resounded with rough gambols and careless clamouring. The hurlyburly even startled a couple of gulls in the trees on the Dike, and Kehlmark, walking up and down with Claudie on the sea-front of the terrace, watched the poor birds frantically revolving for some time, with cries of distress, around the lamp of the lighthouse, and felt for them a sentiment of poetic commiseration, the existence of which his companion did not for a moment suspect. What correlation did he imagine existed between their savage wildness and his own secret anguish. But he quickly roused himself to rattle out a number of empty nothings to the Burgomaster's daughter.

However, the brotherhood of the Guild called for their little bugler, and as he lingered long in the apartments, before the pictures, they went off there to get him, and dragged him away, do what he would, to the extremity of the park. No doubt Henry in his own mind exaggerated their teasing humour towards the young Govaertz, for, as he walked with Claudie, he seemed strangely drawn in the direction of their noisy groups. His approach quietened them and cut short the "ragging" which they were about to inflict upon their victim. Yet, a sort of bashfulness, or fear of men's opinion, prevented Kehlmark from interfering directly in favour of his *protégé*; he turned away and even refrained from speaking to him, but in romping with Claudie he raised his voice, and Guidon artlessly imagined that the Count wished him to hear. At last, the band decided to return to the village. The drum beat the retreat. After a last gathering on the grass, the little barefooted boys of Klaarvatsch ran off to relight their torches. The musicians assumed the head of the procession. The Count conducted them as far as the main gates, and there stood watching them, as to the measured sounds of their favourite march they disappeared down the great elm plantation stretching from the chateau to the village.

Claudie, skipping on to her father's arm, praised the Count of the Dyke to him, or rather lauded his fortune and his luxury, but without as yet confessing to the farmer the great project her mind had conceived.

Little Guidon, with head erect, played his part with unusual bravery. Whilst his bugle seemed to challenge the stars, he was all the time thinking of the master of Escal-Vigor. In the echoes of his music he seemed to hear again the gentle tones of the Dykgrave's voice, and even to see something of his profound look in the velvety darkness. Strange contradiction: notwithstanding this enthusiasm, the poor boy felt his heart swell, his throat tighten, and his eyes ready for tears— and were they sometimes cries of distress, or appeals for help, that his instrument addressed to his distant protector, who still heard them not less overcome with sympathetic distress, long after they died away beneath the exceptionally solemn elms?

IV

B landine, the young woman who unconsciously gave so much umbrage to ambitious Claudie, she whom the Count had styled, not without banter, the "housekeeper," the "steward" of Escal-Vigor, was nearing her thirtieth year. To see her, white, delicate, with reserved manners, features of extreme nobility, a proud melancholy expression, and attired in a neat dress, no one would have ever suspected her humble origin.

Eldest daughter of quite poor peasants, milkmen and kitchen-gardeners, and native, up to her sixteenth year, of one of those rude Flemish provinces, which France, Holland and Belgium share among them, she might have rivalled in exuberance of body and grossness of manners the young farm-girl of Les Pelerins! Her father re-married and, to complete the ill fortune of his little daughter, sole offspring of his first marriage, he did not die before bestowing upon her a number of brothers and sisters. Blandine's stepmother wore her out with work and blows. She was plucky and stoical, a perfect drudge not only did she assist her second mother in the household work, washing, watching over, and attending to the children, but she worked besides in the kitchen-garden, looked after the cows, and went every week on foot to the town to market, laden with pitchers of milk and hampers of vegetables.

In the solitary hours of later years, bent over her sewing, Blandine must have often recalled her native village, and above all her father's thatch-roofed cottage.

This was covered with moss and house-leeks; the weather-eaten walls concealing their cracks behind an entanglement of honeysuckle and wild vine. In the yard the pigs gambolled by the dung-heap, among fowls which they scare and white pigeons which fly away on to the roof, making a plaintive rustle with their wings, a black dog, closely clipped, of the race of *spits*, at once a good watch-dog and a strong beast of burden, was yawning in its kennel, and through the open cat-hole in the stable door two cows might be seen chewing fresh clover.

Blandine will remember for many years yet at Smaragdis the surroundings of the family farm in the Campine land. The Nethe runs not far from there, indulging in truant meanderings, one of its short branches disappears behind the little garden and loses itself in the marshy pastures. The green drevilles, or little alleys of hirsute alders and gibbous willows, which are surrounded in the season by sweet-smelling honeysuckle, accompany like jealous chaperons the course of the silvery stream, which, down below on the borders of the village, turns a water mill, to the great delight of a throng of children.

The manageress of Escal-Vigor recalls, behind the meadows and the farmlands, a melancholy stretch of heath, in the midst of which rises a round hillock, whereon black, unshapely junipers crouched, like an assembly of spooks, like will o'the wisps of the waste, around a solitary beech,—a tree so rare in this region, that a bird of passage alone must have let fall the seed.

This miraculous tree would have been a fitting subject for one of those small figures of the Virgin, placed under glass, on a miniature altar, which simple folk set up, with an astonishing instinct, in the most romantic places in their parishes. This little eminence reminds one of the open air oratory nearby which Joan of Arc heard her "voices."

Little Blandine presented from the most tender age a strange mixture of exalted feeling and intelligence, of sentiment and reason. She had been brought up in the Catholic religion, but, from the days of her catechism had ever refused the strict letter to cleave only to the spirit which gives life.

As she grew older she identified the idea of God with conscience. This may be enough to show that so long as she held the faith her religion had nothing in it of bigotry or cant, but was of a generous and chivalrous character. In Blandine a poetic disposition and fancy was united to a large and honest sense of life. Brave and clever, if she had the imagination of a good fairy, she also had a fairy's industrious fingers.

A woman today, controlling the economy of a lordly domain, she looks back upon herself as a young girl, a little milkmaid, standing in the shadow of the beech which commanded the vast plain of Campine. Blandine hears again the frogs croaking in the ponds and ditches, and her heart delights, as long ago, in the scent of burning newly-clipped wood, that the breeze carries leagues away from those localities. Shepherds' bivouacs, betrayed in the twilight by their spirals of smoke, and at night, by their thin pale flames! Soul of the infinite plain! Barbaric perfume, herald of the region, that none who has once breathed it can ever forget!

It was with this poetry, if somewhat wild and sad, yet hearty and energetic, inspiritress of duty and even of sacrifices aye, and of unknown acts of heroism, that Blandine was impregnated. She was then a small, hard-worked peasant, but one who found time to dream and to wonder, notwithstanding the hard and continual toils to which her stepmother harnessed her.

There was above all one climacteric period which induced in the pseudo-mistress of Escal-Vigor a sort of homesickness for the past: it was towards the twenty-ninth of June, the day of St. Peter and St. Paul, the day on which contracts between masters and servants come to an end.

These transmutations of servants every year serve as pretext for a festival, which Blandine remembers with a sort of voluptuous, soothing melancholy. At Smaragdis, the odour of the elders and syringas was sufficient to call up again before her the circumstances and the actors in these rustic festivities.

A warm sun excites the sweet fragrance of the hedges and thickets. The quail, squatting amid the corn, whines a love-call. No one is any longer working in the freshly-laboured plains. In their haste to go holiday-making, men have thrown down here and there scythe and pruning-bill, hoe and harrow. If the fields are deserted, all along the neighbouring roads on the contrary, there is a long procession of kitchen-gardeners' carts, overhung with white canvas, not laden, as on Fridays, with vegetables and milk, but newly painted, tapestried with flowers, the arches entwined with ribbons, and driven at a good speed by drivers decked out in their Sunday clothes, astonished at their own fine get-up, and in the interior of which are jostled together a crowd of rustic lasses, no less blooming, adorned in their most coquettish attire.

These varlets would come to fetch in the morning, and in a ceremonious manner, the women servants from their former abode, in order to conduct them to the residences of their new masters, and, as the men were not obliged to be at their destination till the evening, they took advantage of the long summer day, to make acquaintance with their future companions in seed-sowing, in field labours, and in harvest.

Often the day-labourers of a parish, the servants of small peasants, borrow a hay-waggon from a large farmer and subscribe for the hire of the horses. All the gangs: thrashers, winnowers, harvestmen, milkmaids, women-haymakers, take their place in the cart, transformed into a perambulating orchard wherein the red puffy faces stand out shining like ruddy apples in the branches.

The fly-net caparisons the cart-horses, for the horse-flies rage all along the oak-drives; but the meshes of the net are hidden under the buttercups, daisies, and roses. Cavalcades are formed. The waggons going to the same villages or returning from the same parishes, jolt along in file, dragging along in company their new legion of servant girls.

A gaudy and noisy defile, a sort of apotheosis of farm-work by the sons of the soil. During their passage the air vibrates with perfume, light, and music.

Cowherds and ploughboys,—the blue smock festooned with a scarlet ribbon, the cap girt with a leafy twig, a branch for goad,—precede the procession like postillions, or else caracole alongside, some astride with short spurs, their legs wide apart owing to the broad backs of their mounts, others seated sideways on the saddle their legs swinging over the horse's left side, just as they may be met in the twilight, going home through narrow path-ways, when the day's work is done.

Their loud voices reverberate from one village to another.

"See there another Roseland!" exclaim the urchins, whom their approach gathers around near the church, for the nickname of "Roseland" has been given to these triumphal cars, on account of the refrain of the ballad sung only by the swains on these occasions:—

> "To the country of roses we wend our way,
> To the land of the rose of a day;
> The flowers so fair like hay we'll mow down,
> And such high stacks make of 'em fine-smelling and gay,
> That the eye, they'll put out, of the man in the moon
> And the sun they'll make sneeze for ever and aye."

Knots of dancers crowd round the doors of the inns. The "Roselanders" invade the bar with a riot like a witches' sabbath. At each stage an enormous watering can is filled with a mixture of beer and sugar and after having taken out the rose, it is passed round from couple to couple.

The girl, assisted by the man accompanying her, moistens her lips the first in the beverage; then, with a gesture derived from the heroic times of old, she bends her body backwards, and with her bared arm, as strong as those of the males, seizes the huge vessel by the handle, brandishes it, raises it above her head, and ends by lowering it to her cavalier.

With one knee on the ground, the thirsty one plunges the pipe of the reservoir in his mouth, and pumps unceasingly, with a face of beatitude, which little Blandine could not help comparing to the ecstasy of communicants receiving the sacrament at solemn festival times. The groups have a fiddler, or an organ-player to accompany them, but indifferent to the melody or rhythm, scraped or ground out, the wenches always dance the same clog-dance, and their voices bray out monotonously the same eternal chorus:

"To the country of roses we wend etc."

To day the serfs are the lords and the poor are the rich.

A whole year's wages resounds against their knee in a pocket as deep as a corn-drill.

Day of good cheer; Fair-day revolutionising the patient priests of the soil! Warm mornings that hatch idylls: stormy evenings that stir up bloodshed!

It is not without reason that the police, from a distance, watch the proceedings of the "Roselanders."

The gendarmes are pale and twist nerously their moustaches, for, as the evening advances, and the time of reaction comes along, these savage and jealous peasants are often the cause of blood-spilling. These goodfellows, drinking freely with every comer, are ready, for a mere nothing, to throw pewter pots at each other's skulls, and to tear each other into rags like so many bantam-cocks. By dint of embracing his neighbour, the demonstrative gossip winds up by pressing him so tightly to his heart as to lug him down to the ground and more than maul him.

The holiday-makers do not all become violent, but all commit acts of folly. They drown their care in beer and stifle it in noise. They drink: some in order to forget, perhaps to relieve the regret they feel at leaving a familiar abode and familiar faces; others, on the contrary, to celebrate their disenfranchisement from the old yoke and to hail, full of confidence, the new fireside.

The greater part fraternise at once with their companions of tomorrow, and lose no time in paying their respects to the gawky females enlisted with them.

And these excellent natures, these irresponsible beings, whom reflection would fatigue, enjoy almost to the verge of licence in a headlong manner, without afterthought and without sparing themselves, the powerful charm of this truce during which they are free in their speech, in their gestures, and of their bodies. They are frantic like dogs let loose, they experience the intoxication that a bird born in a cage must feel when it first flies in the open; and the boundlessness of their felicity makes it almost as poignant as extreme suffering. At times one could not know whether they are weeping, or laughing with tears in their eyes; whether they are fluttering with pleasure, or twisting in convulsions.

As the journey is long, and the day a full one, they stop towards noon before the principal inn of the market town and unyoke the horses. The blouse-clad workmen throw themselves down on the benches in the big room and smoking dishes are placed before them. But in spite of their sharp appetite and the intoxicating joy of their freedom, which vents itself, the livelong day, in rough challenges of ferocious coarseness addressed to God, the Virgin, and the Saints, they neither omit to clasp together their thick callous hands nor to make twice the sign of the cross.

All the sentiments and sensations connected with these festivities were impressed upon the mind of Blandine by the recollection of one of those memorable days of St. Peter and St. Paul. Although only thirteen years old at that time, she suffered more outrages in her own home than the most wretched servant. Her stepmother, either showing by chance a trace of humanity, or perhaps desiring to humiliate her by confounding her with varlets and hirelings, permitted her to take her place in an immense "Roseland," chartered by subscription. The little, chubby-cheeked girl, with eyes of an opaline hue, varying from sky-blue to sea-green, was grateful for her share in these valets and handmaids' amusements; the open good humour of these poor fellows rejoiced her; she enjoyed a childish pleasure at being seated on the flowery and noisy chariot, and at drinking the sugared beer at the stages appointed by the head of the party. The men paid for the beer, the girls furnished the sugaring; Blandine contributed in her turn her share of powdered sugar. She laughed, sang, and danced like her male and female companions. Not thinking of evil, the liberties which were being taken all about her frightened her no more than the twittering of the birds in the trees or the dance of insects in a sunbeam. At the dinner hour she shared the meal of the other Roselanders; afterwards she followed in their train, led away by the atmosphere of good cheer and caresses, feeling herself their little friend, and unable to make up her mind to leave them.

However, towards the evening, a languor, a *morbidesse*, a strange agitation took hold upon her. The kisses and the love-embraces going

GEORGES EEKHOUD

on all around her seemed like the *extravaganza* of a dream. Nothing alarmed her. She found herself in a very agreeable frame of mind.

Night has fallen. Nobody pays any further attention to Blandine. Every servant girl is provided for. But Blandine will have to wait at least three summers before an honest youth would think of her. Her turn will come! That may be what is meant by a certain anticipated homage in the shape of tender glances, or light touches of the body, which some of the gay sparks bestow upon her, as they press slightly against her with their thighs in passing. The child sees no more in the looks, feels no more in the touches than a somewhat rough sympathy, that is all! Around her the tepid air pricks and stimulates their heated bodies. The atmosphere of desire in which they have passed so many hours becomes intensified. Soon Blandine will be unable to recollect the last drinks and sarabands in which she took part. But what enervates her is much more the fermentation of hardy youth a-bustling around her than the scent of roses and the sweet beer. Half-somnambulant, well-nigh swooning from pure felicity, she takes her place with the others in the "Roseland" for the journey homewards, and the chorus ever-more repeated contributes to her half-sleepy condition.

However, across the country, the chariots, roofed over with white canvas, and festooned with flowers, roll along more slowly. The valets and maid-servants hear a rustle and feel something akin to a light equinoctial breeze run along their necks. It is the warm breath of the couples behind them leaning in their direction away on the benches at the back. They sigh; they pant! The little girl falls at last asleep, stupefied by the hot, amorous atmosphere, much more heady than the scent of the hay-fields.

Nobody offers to accompany her home, yet it must surely be time for her to descend from the waggon, and start to get back home, for the others have no thoughts yet of return, and the "Roseland" is still as far from its last stage of pilgrimage as from its last drinking chapel. For, truth to tell, the band of gay sparks know well enough that the real pleasure is now only about to commence.

The company therefore, decides to awaken the little bantling. One of them will set her on her way and then catch up with the Roseland at the next stage. But the girl thanks the complaisant youth and says it is unnecessary for him to trouble himself. She can very well walk alone to her father's cottage. Sometimes, on market days she returns even later, and in what weather and through what roads! The young chap accordingly contents himself with pointing out to her the road she must take,

"Listen, little one, thou'lt cross the heath there, sloping from right to left; then thou'lt reach a fir-grove which thou'lt leave on the right and—"

Blandine hardly heeds him, his voice soon fails to reach her, for she has walked off with a deliberate step. "Good night to all," she cries boldly. Their reply is lost in the cracking of the whip and the noise of the Roseland continuing its road onwards.

Blandine had never felt fear. And then this evening everybody was merry-making. Who would think of doing harm to a child?

Just before, however, at table, after the attack on the grub, they had related plenty of painful, terrifying adventures. Thus, someone expressing surprise that a certain Ariaan, nicknamed the King of Winnowers, long in the service of a farmer of the parish was not of the party, one of the absent man's comrades informed the company that the young fellow had turned out rather badly since their last festival, so badly indeed, that his employer had not thought fit to wait for St. Peter's day to dispense with his services. In spite of all his talents, the King of Winnowers had been dismissed in a hurry for entering into competition with martlets, weasels, polecats and other fanciers of poultry. Not having found a master to whom he could hire his stout arms he had doubtless taken shelter for the time in one or other of those refuges which the generosity of the State opens to dusty feet.

For the sake of form, but not without yawning and stretching, the table uttered a few words of pity for the bad luck of an old companion, such a lively spark too, a good trencher-man, and the rest! But as one of the boys, lighting his pipe, pointed out, it was not the moment to foster black ideas, and so taking his advice, the company made haste to change the subject of conversation.

How happens it that, in crossing the heath, Blandine's thoughts keep obstinately running on the misadventure of the King of Winnowers? Although Ariaan was not wholly unknown to her, he had nothing to do with her in any way. It was a fact that during one season he had dwelt not far from her home. Through the barndoor Blandine used to catch furtive glimpses of him at his work, as he stood there nude to the girdle, ruddy fleshed and humid with moisture but, notwithstanding, attractive in the half-shadow. In measured time the winnowing-fan used to strike his hardened knee, and ended by wearing out his thick breeches, which were always patched in the same place.

Blandine, as she trotted along, left off humming the refrain of the day, to take up that of the winnower!—

Van! Vanne! Vanvarla!
Balle!
Vole!
Vanci! Vanla!

If her heart contracts a little, while she hastens her steps, it is not at all from anxiety for herself, but from a sort of pity for the wastrel. The softened night lends itself to such vague thoughts. The transparent darkness reminds us of dark-hued jewels. There are scintillations in the air, as though the perfumes with which it is saturated have become too vehement and have suddenly taken fire. The intermittent flashes of phosphorescence from the glow-worms harmonise with the chirp-chirp of the crickets.

All at once, while it seems to the belated young girl that the crickets accentuate their irritating music, Blandine is hustled, clasped, and overturned on to a hillock by a human figure, which runs out from behind a broombush. The assailant pulls up her petticoats, forages between her soft, adolescent limbs, handles and strokes her flesh, sighing and panting meanwhile, energetically but not brutally, and finishes by taking entire possession of her.

"Ariaan!" The name, which she would have cried out on recognising the King of the Winnowers, remains stuck in her throat, checked by fright. She experiences a brief pain, like a rending of her belly, and this is followed almost immediately by a strange happiness. Was her being doubled? Endowed with a new sympathy, she was projected out of herself to melt away in an immeasurable sea of delight.

While he holds her under him, she feels herself strongly hypnotised by the expression in the winnower's eyes, and ever afterwards will she associate the mute entreaty in those eyes with the livid sparkling of the glowworms, the scraping of the crickets, the expiring notes of the Roseland chorus, and the rhythm of the old-world song of Ariaan:

Van! Vanne!
Vanci! Vanla!

The night-prowler raised himself from off her, still panting, his breath coming quicker than at his work aforetime, and having helped her to rise in her turn, he held her a few moments by the wrists, gave her a look of gratitude mingled with penitence, and walked away on trembling limbs, adjusting his dress as he went. She never forgot his sorrel face nor the zigzags that his silhouette traced in the motionless space into which he finally disappeared.

Blandine dragged herself, more distressed than indignant, towards her home, and on going to bed, she vowed to herself never to reveal what had happened to her. An instinct of solidarity more than of modesty dictated this silence. In truth, she could not bring herself to be angry with this ruffian, at first so commanding, and then so dejected, almost sheepish; she was persuaded even, that he would have asked pardon, had he dared, but tenderness and a certain gratitude made him almost as timid as violent desire had rendered him unbridled. A few days later Blandine heard that big Ariaan had been arrested in the environs, captured by the police as he was swimming across the Nethe. Her pitiable violator had become a formidable criminal. She was resolved more than ever to keep silence, anxious not to involve him in new difficulties or to bring upon him a heavier punishment.

But the unfortunate girl had counted without considering the tell-tale denunciations of nature. She became pregnant.

Her stepmother, pharisaically virtuous, burst out into loud outcries, tore her hair, pretended to be in despair; but inwardly she was delighted with this plausible occasion to rage against her victim, and to give free course to her unnatural instincts.

Perhaps even, in sending this child with the Roseland had she hoped some such thing might happen.

"Day of judgment and damnation!" shouted the vixen. "Shame and treble scandal! Our good name gone for ever! Double-dyed whore! What an example for thy brothers and sisters! It is a good thing for thee that thy good honest father is dead. He would have ripped thee open like the bitch thou art."

She demanded full information. "His name? Tell me his name." "Never; do forgive me for not obeying thee, mother."

"His name? Out with it! Wilt thou not speak?" A blow followed. Then a second.

"His name?" "No, Mother!"

"Thou refusest! Ah! we'll see about that! His name I say? For he's got to marry thee." "Nay, thou would'st not have him for son-in-law, Mother."

"Thou rotten swine? Thou admit'st thyself that he's no good. He is then so low, thy gallant, that we, lousy as we are, are too decent for him? But it's all very fine talking of marriage. The villain who has debauched thee shall have rather a taste of prison, for thou'rt a minor, although marriageable, and as precocious as a gutter cat. Let us see! It is no doubt one of the Roselanders; some drunken swineherd, who must have taken thee for his favourite sow. Don't hope to save him, for the magistrates will soon wring a confession out of him, or his own comrades will sell him in the end."

This time she replied with courage and not without pity:

"No, 'twas none of the Roselanders. It was a poor man, a passer-by more miserable than any of them. I had never seen him before and he does not even belong to these parts. He was sad, it seemed to me; one of those to whom we are glad to give alms. I would not have refused him aught, but I did not even know till these last days what I had granted him."

"Thou two-faced hypocrite, thou liest!"

The fury rained more blows on the unfortunate, ordering her at each blow to speak; then, as Blandine persisted in her refusal, she fell upon her with fists and feet. To support her courage under this treatment Blandine with a smile on her lips recalled to her mind the tall youth with the bronze complexion and the sad, beseeching eyes. She found it sweet to bear hardship for the sake of this hunted outcast. The stepmother dragged her along the ground, utterly exasperated at so much calmness.

Then, indifferent to suffering and obstinate in her self-sacrifice, Blandine began to sing the *Ave Maris Stella*, one of the canticles for the month of May. Under the blows which rained upon her, the child recalled to her memory the dry sound of the fan on Ariaan's knee. Fainting, but morally unconquerable, she mixed the two songs, the church canticle and the labourer's song, and closing her eyes she confounded in one fervent memory the fumes of incense and the dust arising from the fan, the perfumes of the church with the odour of the rustic's sweat:—

Van! . . . Vanne! . . . Vanvarla!
Balle! . . . Vole! . . . Vanci! . . . Vanla!
Vanne! . . . Ave. . . Maris. . . Stella!

Seeing her covered with blood, the wretch dragged her into the pigsty, shut her up there, making one of the children take her a pitcher of water and a chunk of bread. The next day the rough market-woman endeavoured to return to the charge, but she would have herself broken down sooner than succeed in wresting from Blandine what she wished to know.

Weary of the struggle, the virtuous *paysanne* induced the vicar to try what he could do. This gentleman was paternal and wheedling:

"What is all this about little Blandine? Must I believe what thy worthy mother tells me? Thou'rt not going to be naughty! . . . Thou'rt rebellious? After having sinned thou'lt not name thy accomplice? . . . Ah, that is bad, very bad!"

"Father, I have confessed my wrong to my mother and am ready to confess it to you, but betraying others is hateful to me."

"That's all very well, my daughter! How high and mighty we do get! And if I thy pastor were of opinion that thou ought to give up to us the name of this evildoer."

"I would refuse, all the same, *Monsieur le Curé.*"

And, as the priest, quite taken aback at such insubordination, shot a severe glance at her, Blandine burst into sobs, exclaiming."

"Yes, I would refuse *Monsieur le Curé*, I would not even tell this name to the good God if he did not know it. This man is already unhappy enough. To name him would bring him into further trouble. They would keep him longer in prison on my account."

The innocent child had during the last few days been greatly enlightened as to human laws and the conventions of right and wrong.

"But," objected the priest, "dost thou love this wretched fellow?" "I do not know if I love him; but I do not hate him at all."

"He has, however, done thee wrong, my child."

"Perhaps! I am willing to believe it even, since you say so, but *Monsieur le Curé*, is it not said in the catechism that we must forgive our enemies and cherish even those who hate us?"

The priest raged inwardly, but no longer insisted.

Then the peasant woman curious and salacious, changing her tactics, wished at least to know if the child had been taken by force.

Blandine, in order the better to throw the blood-hounds of the law off the scent, and to palliate the poor fellow's offence, pretended not to have tried to escape from his attempt.

But, for a moment, seeing that her cruel step-mother persisted in suspecting one or another of the Roselanders, poor Blandine felt grievous scruples. In refusing to reveal the name of the real culprit, was she not exposing those brave chaps to being troubled if not to being found perhaps guilty? Fortunately, it was easy for all of them to prove their perfect innocence.

The worthy fellows were extremely sorry for her misadventure, especially the one who had offered to see her home, and who blamed himself now for not having accompanied her in spite of herself.

Sometimes the high-minded child cherished a desire to start and seek out the man who had dishonoured her, and who dared not make reparation, not only because he had committed a crime in the eyes of men, but because in the opinion of the public the condition of a bastard and of an unwedded mother would be better than that of the legal son and the lawful companion of a thief and a vagabond. Blandine, more and more elevated in spirit, felt herself strong enough to go in the teeth of any unjust convention, whether religious or social. Since that fatal day of Saints Peter and Paul her heart had vowed itself to a stern and exacting vocation of devotion and self-sacrifice.

She had made up her mind she would go to the prison. She would see Ariaan in order to pardon him. She would free him from guilt by a sublime falsehood; lay the burden on her own shoulders, say she had surrendered herself to him voluntarily and had concealed her true age. Developed as she was, Ariaan might easily have believed in all good faith that he had seduced a girl who had attained her majority.

So it was decided. She would accept to be the wife of a thief and a jail-bird. . .

But what mysterious presentiment stopped the young girl in her charitable impulse, and made her understand that her hour was not yet come, and that a being, wretched and anathematised in a far different way from the simple poultry-thief, was waiting for her somewhere?

While she still hesitated and doubtful battles were waging in her heart, an event happened, that rendered any sacrifice, for the time being at least, unnecessary:—Blandine brought into the world a dead child.

This climax disarmed the rancour of the parish and cut short the scandal. Her fault being in this manner expiated, the stepmother treated the poor girl with less barbarity. Her brothers and sisters ceased to torment Blandine and to keep her at a distance like an ill-odoured animal. Her services were accepted and she obtained the favor of being allowed to exert herself for the benefit of the family. Some time after that her step-mother died.

Blandine, at that time fifteen years of age, showed herself of decidedly heroic stamp, although simple in character. She took into her hands the control of the household, busied herself over its multifarious needs, assumed all responsibilities and cares, and looked after the children, not resting until they were all advantageously placed out, the boys as apprentices and the girls as domestic servants. So well did the valiant little mother work that she found her character more than rehabilitated. The first was the parish priest, who could not make it out; his admiration of her was mingled with a sort of stupefaction. The pluck and sturdy character of this brat of a girl quite confused him.

V

About this time the Dowager of Kehlmark, having given up her troublesome establishment and retinue of servants, to retire into a pleasant villa in an aristocratic suburb of the capital, was seeking for a trustworthy young person, something between a lady-companion and a waiting woman. One of her old friends, passing the summer at Blandine's village, spoke of the girl highly, even at the vicar's request, to the great lady, without omitting to mention the adventure of which she had once been the victim. It turned out that that particular account of the poor girl's past proved the means of winning her the sympathies of Henry's grandmother, who engaged her immediately she was presented.

But what a graceful and polished village-girl! She was the picture of health and uprightness. The contour of a modernised Greek statue vivified by rosy cheeks; eyes, limpid and trusting, of clear sapphire blue; a mouth curved gracefully and with a touch of melancholy; somewhat curly hair, of a light ash hue, parted in two halves on a forehead of immaculate ivory. Of moderate stature and admirable proportions, in her peasant dress she might have passed for a young lady of quality masquerading as a shepherdess.

On her side, Blandine felt herself drawn to this septuagenarian lady, who, though of noble family, was free from haughtiness and affectation, and would not have been out of place, by reason of her philosophical bent, in the days of Diderot and the Encyclopedia. A woman of liberal culture and without prejudices, if she still retained some feeling of pride in her aristocratic birth, it was because, in comparing herself with the upstarts who surrounded her, she was compelled to recognize the superiority in sentiments, tone and education of a caste ever decreasing in numbers, and even more reduced and proscribed by the puddled blood of financial misalliances than by the guillotine and September massacres. But, on the other hand, she considered as a truly aristocratic appanage those high qualities of heart and mind which are to be met with in every walk of life, and the possession of which was equivalent with her to letters patent, taking the place, to a large extent, of a genealogical tree.

Malvina de Kehlmark, *née* De Taxandrie, whose former striking beauty the "Almanac of the Muses" in 1830 proclaimed as Ossianic, possessed lively eyes of azure grey, whose iridescence could be compared only to superfine pearls, hair that hung English-wise in ringlets, an elegantly arched nose, and lips teeming with wit. She was tall and lithe, with the carriage of a queen, or in painters' parlance a splendid outline, rendered more impressive by trailing velvet or black satin robes, with wide lace sleeves, caps *à la Marie Stuart*: a rich but reserved costume, in which the carbuncles of her rings and especially her brooch, a sphinx-head cut in onyx and surmounted with a *couronne* of diamonds and rubies, shone like constellations.

In this majestic woman was nothing of pedantry or affected gravity; she was neither prude nor vulgar; but good, without being priggish, and even with a touch of brusqueness and banter; affectionate, faithful, and of infinite sensibility; by no means a Pharisee, she abhorred nothing but treachery, duplicity, and baseness of soul.

Such an evangelical freethinker was bound infallibly to agree with an equally very dissenting Christian. The Dowager laughed, not ill-naturedly, at what she called the mummeries of Blandine, but in no way interfered with her in the practice of her religion, which, indeed, was on a very reduced scale. With her gay, optimistic, critical disposition, Madame de Kehlmark formed a striking contrast with the prematurely reflective and hardened character of the young girl, whom she nicknamed her little Minerva, her Pallas Athene.

The old lady amused herself by instructing her, and taught her so well to read and write that she made her at last her reader and secretary.

But she instilled into the girl above all things a devotion to her grandson, her Henry, who was then studying at Bodemberg Schloss, and of whom Madame de Kehlmark said archly, that he was her only prejudice, her superstition, her fanaticism. Without ceasing, she talked to her young companion of this little prodigy, this precocious child. She read and read over to her again the schoolboy's letters. Blandine replied to them under the grandmother's dictation; but very often she was the first to find the affectionate word, or turn of phrase, which the old lady was seeking. She finally wound up by writing the whole epistle straight off the reel, according to the sketch which she asked for from her mistress, the latter confessing that Blandine's style was even more maternal than her own.

The Dowager also showed her the portraits of the young Count, and the two women would go over for hours, without weariness, the various pictures of their fetish, from the daguerreotype which represented him as a restless baby with one foot bare, on his mother's knees, up to the most recent proof showing a slender youth, with two big wide-staring eyes, at his first communion.

At the outset, Blandine only pretended to interest herself in everything which concerned the little Kehlmark, and would herself start the conversation about him, solely to please the excellent woman and flatter her touching solicitude, but, by degrees, she was surprised to find herself sharing this worship of the absent boy. She cherished him deeply in her heart even before she had seen him. It will be observed in the sequel that there was in this attachment a profounder and more providential influence than that of a simple case of auto-suggestion.

"How tall he must be now! And strong! And handsome!" the two women would surmise. They described him to each other mutually, the one supplying flattering retouches to the image that the other sketched. How Blandine longed to see him! She even languished in waiting. And lo! bad news comes from Switzerland at the moment of the vacations which were to send him back to his grandmother. Henry had fallen ill. Never had Blandine known such misgivings. She would have flown to the schoolboy's bed, had she not been detained by the side of his grandparent, hanging between life and death as long as her grandson was in danger. Then what jubilation when Blandine learned the recovery of the young man!

The prospect of the return to his country home of this pampered child rendered Blandine not the less anxious of the two women. She counted the days and even, in a sort of puerile way, struck them out on the calendar as they passed, just as the boy himself was doubtless doing at school.

When Henry rang at the villa gate it was Blandine who opened the door to him. She thought she beheld a god! All her blood rushed back to her heart. She adored him at first sight, respectfully with no self-interested hope, or ambition for herself, understanding that in living ever in the presence of the young Kehlmark, she would have her full desire, the complete aim of her aspirations. Later, she better understood what had passed within her at this first and decisive meeting. Therefore, her complex impression can only become really definite through the successive phases of this narrative. In short, the pious Blandine was strongly affected by Henry. Into this climax of feeling, towards which her sympathies had long been directed, there was mingled fear, anguish and admiration, perhaps even a little of that secret pity, which we experience in the presence of things rare, ephemeral, and almost incompatible with ordinary life.

"It is Mademoiselle Blandine, doubtless, the little fairy, whom my good grandmamma has praised to me so highly," said the young man, extending his hand to the lady's companion. "I am very, very grateful to you for all your care of her," he added, with a little timidity.

The two young people were not long before they treated each other on a footing of comradeship. Under a frolicsome manner, Blandine concealed the deep and serious love which possessed her. Was it because she knew herself won to Kehlmark for life that she had no recourse to any of those artful manœuvres by which a woman binds a lover to her side. Her absence of coquetry contributed to put the timid and whimsical youth at his ease, unused as he was to poses of gallantry. Some days there were when he showed himself particularly attentive, whilst on others he looked at her strangely, and seemed to avoid, and even to flee from her.

Three years elapsed. It was in the month of May and the day was drawing to a close. The Dowager of Kehlmark was dining out alone, at the house of her old friend, Madame de Gasterlé, as was her custom once a month. Blandine was to call for her at this lady's, near the stroke of ten o'clock. Henry had retired to his room where he was working,— or rather pretending to work, for the moment and the season of the year produced an enervating effect, exciting him to fancies and curious imaginations.

Through the open window the young Count hears the sound of organs and accordions coming from a workmen's quarter, across some acres of cultivated gardens, distributed between the dowager's villa and those of her neighbours, and divided from each other by bright green hedges. For several evenings the plaintive strains of brass-bellied instruments calling "all lights out" in an artillery barracks situated away down at the further extremity of the faubourg, had come, wafted along on the warm breeze to Kehlmark's ears, mingled with the music of the lilies that agitated their fragrant-tipped thyrses.

There was also building a-going on in the neighbourhood: the principal construction is on the morrow to receive its roof, and throughout the day the young patrician has heard the silvery music made by the masons as they strike the bricks with their trowels. Several times, feeling disturbed, he has leaned out and has seen the labourers, covered with white dust and wild of aspect, pretty country boys, with trough or hod on shoulder, unconscious balancers, mount up the high scaffoldings and risk the giddiness of lofty ascent. At times they remain masked by the foliage, then all on a sudden they emerge from behind the tall-grown trees, their active bodies standing out in dramatic silhouette against the neutral blue of the sky.

Why does his heart swell with indescribable nostalgia, when, after sunset, he sees them pass the rustic blue smock over their work-a-day clothes as daubed and besmeared as a painter's palette? It will be still worse the day after tomorrow when they will have finished; their harmonious activity, like an orchestra, was becoming an habitual pleasure to his eyes, and he foresees that he will miss them, these toilers, especially one, an alert, light-haired youth, who was better made, had finer curves than the others, and whose supple and statuesque movements of the hips, calves, and shoulders would have driven a sculptor to despair.

"Some of these masons' assistants will be withdrawn later from their decorative trade to serve in the barracks," Kehlmark reflects, when he heard the calls of the clarion, meant one day for them, die away in a quaking of leaves and a stirring of fragrant odours. Workmen, peasants, torn from their villages, soldiers in barracks, ardently longing after their villages far away, sharp-pointed steeples which rend your heart with homesickness:—this association of fugitive ideas in Kehlmark's mind turned into one dominant idea of the peasant, from whence stood out all at once, as though symbolic, the image of Blandine, not at all the Blandine of the present day, but the little peasant girl, such as she seemed retrospectively to him, the poet enamoured of strength and simple nature.

"She is upstairs at her toilette," he said to himself, "for it is nearly time for her to join grandmamma."

Somnambulistic, his eyes blinded with rustic licence and desperate embracings, he ascended the stairs to the young girl's room.

Although she was in her chemise Blandine only experienced a slight shiver, scarcely perceptible, at this intrusion. It was as though she had expected him. In the act of combing out her luxuriant head of hair, which was flowing over her shoulders, and wafting forth the scent of lavender and other fragrant herbs of the country, she turned towards him with a trusting smile. He took her by the hands, but almost without looking at her, as though scrutinising things absent, or at a distance, even closing his eyes to fathom these baffling scenes; and pushed her, unresisting, without a word, towards the bed which had just been remade. She, quivering and ravished, continued to smile, and surrendered herself as though to a new vagabond.

Why did he recollect, before the spasm, the accordion music in the twilight, across the lilac-flowers in bloom and the youthful villagers putting on their blue smocks over their faded working clothes? Was it because these country lads might have come from his mistress's village? He gloried to be in touch through her with an entire rustic humanity; it was the strength, the savour, the rough and carnal gesture, the fleshly passion redolent of the soil, which he loved in Blandine on this nuptial evening. This time, as well as those that followed, he possessed her in the thought of the desires which she would have excited in sturdy rural labourers, who might embrace her in one of those impetuous, savage onslaughts, smoking hot, with clothes all undone and wind-tost, that took place in the priapic orgies of the annual Fair.

During a moment, Blandine had caught the look in his half-open eyes. What abyss did she discover there? The abyss attracts, and love is partly made up of dizziness. Without abandoning herself to the fulness of the joy which she had hoped for, without swooning as in the midst of the phosphorescent heather, in the arms of the King of the Winnowers, she felt throughout her being a tenderness more tragic for the young Count of Kehlmark. She had surprised in Henry's expression an infinite anguish, in his embrace the tight clinging of a drowning person, in his kiss the suffocation of a man being murdered, who cries for help.

She had given herself up to him, dominated by his superiority of mind; and she was always respectful and humble in their relations. Ariaan, that fine healthy brute, had never, Blandine was now convinced, been consumed with erotic terrors comparable to those which stirred the flesh and the imagination of this too intellectual and too speculative young patrician.

While worshipping him absolutely, she always approached him with a certain disquietude, like the shivering of the swimmer at his first contact with the water. She found him strange, fantastic, almost terrifying. At times, there seemed to hang about him a sadness like that of a melancholy landscape; he was dull and sombre like a canal traversing a district encumbered with gravel and ash. The gloom, which thus intermittently weighed upon his mind passed like a film over his fine blue eyes. At the very height of his accesses of kindness and tenderness occurred reactions, chilliness, sudden shrinkings. His character seemed drawn-and-quartered by continual set-backs. No matter, from the first

GEORGES EEKHOUD

appearance of Kehlmark she felt herself in the presence of a mysterious being in whom spoke an unknown voice, which would always thrill her; she had vowed herself to him without hope of salvation as to a god who would banish her eternally far from his paradise, and when she looked at him there was in her eyes the expression of a martyr vainly searching the skies for the flight of angels that should come and deliver him. And yet, she was still ignorant of the rites and the worst trials of the religion of love to which she had consecrated herself.

VI

The season of their carnal love did not last long. When the bonds of their physical union were relaxed and then dissolved, Blandine was but little afflicted and hardly surprised. However, she loved him more passionately than ever, cherishing an idolatrous gratitude for the homage which he had paid her, and esteeming herself happy and proud in his attachment.

The Dowager had suspected their good understanding, but she was ignorant how far their love had gone. She smiled benignly on this affection, for she became more and more accustomed to look upon Blandine as her granddaughter, and as the sister, if not the wife of her Henry.

Madame de Kehlmark herself admired her grandson, but being clear-sighted and her very solicitude making her acute, she divined that he was exceptional even to the extent of anomaly; and something whispered to her also that the young Count would be unhappy, if he was not already so. She was alarmed at the readiness, or rather, at the restlessness of his genius. He would work by fits and starts, would shut himself up in his apartment and remain there for weeks without seeing the streets, reading, rhyming, composing scores, saturating himself with the spirit of Beethoven, Schumann and Wagner, daubing canvas, arranging his papers; then afterwards, to these times of excessive confinement, succeeded periods in which he experienced an imperious need to play the fool, when he would take pleasure in frequenting the suspicious quarters of the town, in exploring the low lodging-houses of sailors and boatmen, giving himself up to unbridled night-wanderings, disappearing for several days, passing entire carnivals without seeing his bed, and when at last he came to throw himself down on it like jetsam thrown on the beach, or like a wounded, hunted deer, which has succeeded in reaching its lair, spent and exhausted, it was to go out no more for several days, and to sleep, sleep, and sleep again!

The reader may imagine the nightmare through which the two women passed. Generally they had no idea what had become of him. In setting out on these excursions he took care not to say where he was going, just as on his return he kept silence as to how he had passed his time and what the things were that possessed him. How reconcile such out-breakings with the filial devotion which he entertained for his grandmother! On his return from these expeditions he would weep like a child and would beg the good lady's pardon, but would say, it was beyond his power to do otherwise; this change, this tumultuous diversion was necessary to him; he felt a need to play the fool, to intoxicate himself with movement and noise, in order to drive away God knows what preoccupation; for on that point he refused to explain himself. Or else, he would allege headaches or neuralgia, the remains of his serious illness of former days at the boarding-school.

It happened one day that, at the request of Madame de Kehlmark, he conducted Blandine to the gayest ball of the season. Towards dawn, he took her under cover of the domino into the public dancing-halls of a far lower class, presented her to any chance masks they encountered, and made her play her part in villainous pleasures, in an atmosphere which inebriated him like bad alcohol, but without procuring for him joy nor even the illusion of joy. It was remarked of him in the town that he no longer associated with people of his own class, but that on the contrary, he sought the society of needy artists and men of letters, or even of the lowest parasites. Disregarding etiquette and the worldly code, he did not show himself in any drawing-room.

His tastes and inclinations presented strange contradictions. Thus the same dilettante who collected rare stamps and cherished costly bound volumes, made a collection of the cast-off clothes and the tools of poor workingmen, of sailors' knives, and of soiled suburban-ball entry-tickets.

After having shown himself so very expansive, the young Count wrapped himself up in a sort of savage constraint. Even his joy was out of tune, a hoarse intonation of voice revealing gloomy, hidden thoughts, to such a degree that Blandine long doubted whether he had ever known a day of real serenity. If he tried to express pleasure he only grimaced; his smile looked more like a grinding of the teeth. He seemed to carry within him that bitter smoke whereof Dante speaks: *Portando dentro accidioso fummo*. He looked as though he wished to stifle a secret pain, to silence one knew not what remorse! In his large ultramarine eyes, there was often something provocative and offensive, but when he omitted to compose his face, the same eyes were full of that boundless agony that Blandine had once caught there, and which had produced upon her a lifelong impression, an agony like the terror of a beast at bay, of a condemned man ascending the scaffold, or better still, like the aspect, at once sublime and sinister, of a Prometheus, a stealer of forbidden fire.

Liberal even to prodigality, passionate for righteous causes, revolted by the rascalities of the multitude, sensitive to excess, he arrived at a point where he could not suffer contradiction and fell into a rage with anyone who attempted to thwart him. Thus, one day when Blandine wished to take from him a pretty child, the offspring of some poor people on a visit to Madame de Kehlmark, and for whom Henry had conceived a tenderness, he so far forgot himself as to pursue his friend with a dagger and even to wound her in the shoulder. A reaction immediately followed and, mad with despair and horrified at his own conduct, he threatened to turn against himself the weapon which he had directed against Blandine.

Justly alarmed at this terrifying episode, the Dowager contrived, unknown to her grandson so as to avoid exciting his wrath, to bring about an interview with a celebrated practitioner, who came to the villa on the pretext of requesting from Kehlmark information on some bibliophilistic point. The physician studied the young man for a long time, under cover of a conversation concerning scientific literature.

In his report to the Countess, the doctor diagnosed a nervous irritability, the cause of which he laboured in vain to discover. At all events, he prescribed a hydropathic treatment and physical exercises,—swimming, fencing, skating, riding,—and declared, for the rest, that he had discovered in the subject no organic lesion or any morbid defect. On the contrary, he asserted that he had never encountered a more active intelligence, so sane a judgment, or an equal elevation of views in so vivacious a nature; and he ended by congratulating the grandmother, saying, with rough professional bluntness:—

"Madame, either I am a perfect ass, or this high-spirited young fellow will do honour to your name. He has genius, your grandson; he is of the stamp of those from whom the Future recruits her artists, conquerors and apostles!"

"Ah! would that he were rather of the stamp of those elected to happiness!" sighed the Dowager, but little ambitious, although of course, flattered by these predictions of glory.

VII

Whilst awaiting the fulfilment of these brilliant prognostications, Kehlmark applied himself again to those athletic exercises in which he had excelled at the boarding-school. Unfortunately, he brought to these sports the same fever and extravagance he put into his words and actions. He took pleasure in breakneck exploits, in swimming across broad rivers, in sailing boats in stormy weather, and in breaking in restive and vicious horses. One day his horse ran away, and galloped all along the railway, keeping head with an express train, side by side with the locomotive, until falling down exhausted, it dragged its rider under it. Kehlmark escaped with a sprain. Another time the same horse, whose recklessness was extreme, being then harnessed to a dog-cart, took offence at a mason's wheelbarrow, left in the middle of the street, and after a terrifying shy, took to a frantic gallop across a square planted with trees, until at last it dashed itself, together with the carriage, against a street-lamp. Kehlmark and his groom were pitched head over heels, but they immediately stood up again on their feet without a scratch. The horse also escaped unhurt by the collision. As for the carriage, which was broken up and twisted, a lounger was induced by a tip to wheel it as far as the coachmaker's. A merchant of the neighbourhood hastened to place his horse and carriage at the disposal of Monsieur de Kehlmark. It was about nightfall, the Dowager was expecting Henry for dinner, and he was far from home. The groom drew his master's attention to the very excited condition of the horse, which pricked up its ears, kept on snorting from fright and was trembling all over, and advised him to accept the gentleman's offer. But the Count only agreed to borrow the carriage. The fiery animal was harnessed to the merchant's carriage. Kehlmark resumed the reins, and the groom took his place on the box but not without surliness. Contrary to their expectation, the horse seemed calmed and behaved in an ordinary manner.

But in passing over a viaduct not far from the station, they noticed, below the flight of steps, a crowd of people excited at a train blazing with ignited petroleum, which shot forth flames as high as houses.

"Look, Monsieur le Comte, that will set him mad again! If I were you I would again turn about," suggested Landrillon, the servant. And he was about to descend.

But Henry prevented him, whipping up the horse and giving it the reins so that the scared animal started trotting across the crowd.

"*A la grâce de Dieu!*" exclaimed the Count with a disdainful smile.

Disappointing the alarmed anticipations of the valet, the animal, which a bit of paper or a dead leaf was generally sufficient to terrify, passed through the crowd, and trotted, without showing the least panic, through the midst of the crackling flames, the whistling of the water from the steam-pumps, and the cries and tumult of the spectators.

"All the same, Monsieur, we have escaped it finely!" said Landrillon when they had passed the critical zone. And he grumbled spitefully between his teeth:—

"With such antics as these he will one day wind up by leaving his skin behind. That's his business, but what right has he to risk my bones as well?"

It might be thought indeed that the Count was seeking occasions to do himself an injury. With what trouble could he be afflicted thus to despise the life which two loving women strove to render sweet and bright for him?

The Countess and Blandine were just now passing through agonies even more painful than before. The poor, old grandmother hoped, by gratifying his most expensive whims, to reconcile him to existence, but at the rate he was going he would, in the end, ruin himself both in health and fortune. "What will become of him when I am no more?" the good woman wondered. "He will have need, indeed, of a loving and prudent companion, a woman of good management, a guardian angel of profound and absolute devotion."

Out of respect for certain prejudices still remaining, Madame de Kehlmark would not go so far as to recommend marriage to those whom she called her two children, but all the same, she would not in any way have dissuaded them from it. When she was alone with Blandine she expressed her apprehensions for the young Count's future: "This big boy, full of illusions, will need a veritable angel, to serve him as a guide, and to conduct him through life; someone who, without snatching him roughly from his chimeras, will lead him gently by the hand into paths of reality."

Blandine promised her benefactress, with all her heart, to watch always over the young Count and never to leave him unless he drove her away. The Dowager would have gladly made their union indissoluble, but she dared not approach this delicate subject with Henry or communicate to him her dearest wish. Anxiety of mind at length affected her robust health and her state grew worse from day to day. She saw death approach with that proud resignation which she had imbibed from the works of her favourite philosophers; she would even have welcomed it with the joy that a worker, overcome by the fatigue of a hard week, shows at the approach of the Sunday's rest, if the fate of her dear boy had not stricken her with anguish.

Henry and Blandine were standing at her bedside, deceived by the calmness of the dying woman, and unable to believe in the imminence of her end. It would appear that the nearness of death confers on the sufferers the gift of second-sight and of prophecy. Did the Dowager of Kehlmark have a glimpse of the scabrous future in store for her grandson? Did she fear to ask Blandine to associate her destiny irrevocably with Henry's? At all events, she never gave expression to her supreme desire. With a smile full of unspeakable adjuration, she contented herself with pressing their joined hands together, as though performing a sacramental act, and passed away, grieving not at death, but at having to leave her children.

By her will she left to Blandine a sufficiently large sum to ensure her independence and to permit her to set up a house of her own. But, even if she had not promised it to the deeply venerated dead, the young woman would have remained for life with Henry de Kehlmark.

When, some months after the grandmother's death, Henry more and more disgusted with the banal and conventional world, announced to Blandine his intention of establishing himself at Escal-Vigor, far from the capital, in a fertile and barbarous island, she replied simply:

"That suits me perfectly, Monsieur Henry."

Notwithstanding their intimacy,she seldom omitted this respectful prefix before the young man's name.

Kehlmark, not having yet sounded the depth of the absolute affection which she devoted to him, had imagined that she would take advantage of the liberality of the deceased to return to her native country of Campine, and seek there a suitable husband.

"What do you mean?" he asked her, intimidated by the air of grieved surprise, which had overcast the young woman's countenance.

"With your permission, Monsieur Henry, I will follow you wherever you think it well to settle, unless my presence has become troublesome to you."

And reproachful tears fluttered on her trembling eye-lashes, although she made an effort to smile at him as usual.

"Forgive me, Blandine," stammered the awkward young man. "You know very well that no company, no presence, could be more welcome to me than yours. But still I do not want to abuse your self-devotion. After having sacrificed some of the best years of your youth to the care of my venerable grandmother, I cannot consent for you to bury yourself down there in a desert with me; in a false situation, exposed to the slanders of ill-disposed rustics; much less can I agree to it now, when you are free, the dear departed having endeavoured to recognise your devoted services by assuring to you an independence. You can therefore establish yourself advantageously."

He was going to add "and find a husband," but the eyes of his mistress, more and more in tears, made him aware that such a speech would have been abominable.

"Yes," he continued, taking her hands and looking at her with those enigmatic eyes, in which there was at once uneasiness and excitement, "you deserve to be happy, very happy, my good Blandine. For you were so affectionate, even better than I, her grandson, to the beloved dead. Ah! I occasioned her much anxiety—you know something about it, you, her confidant.—I caused her anguish in spite of myself, but cruelly, all the same. And perhaps, by my unsteady character and numerous extravagances I hastened her end. But believe me, Blandine, it was not my fault; I never did it on purpose. There were other things that caused it, things that nobody, not even you, could understand or imagine; a certain fatality, something inexplicable, was mixed up with it."

Here his look became still more cloudy, and with the back of his hand he wiped the perspiration off his forehead, no doubt regretting that he could not at the same time wipe from his brain the thought that oppressed him.

"Whilst you, Blandine," he added, "you were always pure balm to her, nothing but smiles and caresses. Ah, leave me, my poor child, the time has come to separate; it will be better for you, if not for me."

He turned aside, quite overcome, ready to weep himself, and was going away, waving her off with a gesture; but she eagerly seized upon the hand that thought to banish her.

"You do not really wish it, Henry," she cried with a voice of entreaty that pierced the young Count to the heart. "Where should I go to? After your sainted grandmother no one but you remains for me to cherish. You are the only motive of my existence. And above all do not talk to me of sacrifice. The years which I had the honour of passing with Madame de Kehlmark could never have been happier. I owe everything to your grandmother, Count. 0 suffer me humbly to repay to you the debt which I owe her! You will have need of a manager, a steward, to take charge of your affairs, manage your fortune, and direct your household. You entertain ideas too noble, too brilliant, for you to weary yourself with these prosaic and material details. Counting and reckoning is not in your line; as for me, it is my life. That indeed, is all 1 know. Now Monsieur Artist" (she became adorably wheedling), "here is a good suggestion: do not send me away this time; agree to keep me on in the employment which I filled with the Countess. If she were here she would herself intercede for me.—Unless you think of marrying!"

"I marry!" he cried. "I marry!"

It was impossible to mistake the intonation of these words. The Count of Kehlmark was evidently much averse to any matrimonial compact whatsoever.

Blandine could hardly conceal her joy; she laughed through her tears.

"Well, Henry, in that case I will never leave you. Who will look after your great château down there? Who will take care of you? Is there anyone who knows your tastes better than I do, or who is so careful to satisfy them? No, Henry, separation is impossible. You could no more do without me than I could banish myself from your presence. Even if you had married, I would have wished to live at your fireside in a corner, unnoticed, submissive, nothing but your humble servant. Yes, if you desire it, I will be nothing more than your faithful factotum. Ah, Monsieur Henry, take me with you; you will see I shall be hardly an encumbrance, I will never weary you with my presence, I will efface myself as much as you require. Besides, I can truly say, Henry, it was your grandmother's wish; keep me at least for the sake of the dear one who has gone."

And deeply moved, Blandine burst anew into sobs; Kehlmark also felt himself shaken to the depths of his heart. He drew the young girl gently to his bosom and gave her a brotherly kiss on the forehead.

"Well, let it be as you wish," he murmured, "but may you never repent of it and never reproach me with this fatal consent!"

In speaking these last words his voice trembled, and became smothered, as though conscious of the menace of an inevitable catastrophe.

VIII

Together with Blandine, the Count had taken with him to Escal-Vigor his only servant, the same who had accompanied him at the time of the carriage accident.

Thibaut Landrillon, son of an Ardennes forest guard, was a solid, squat, thick-set man, not badly made. Having passed a long time in barracks he had retained something of the reveller and the libertine, a "breaker of dishes and of hearts," as he used to say, in his jargon of the guard-room. His face was round, his eyes brown and very sharp and lively, having in them a sort of moist expression of lubricity; he had a small nervous nose, like a King Charles pug-dog, thick lips of the hue of red lead, the sign at once of cruelty and sensuality; a slight moustache; reddish cheeks with a menacing look of inflammation about them; small, hairy satyr's ears; hair coarse, like brushwood; his style of talking was thick and bantering; his hips rolling, his legs crooked. A free-liver of a low class, he concealed under an appearance of rough honesty and an affected air of goodfellowship, a rapacious and crafty spirit.

His scurrilous manners, his vulgar and sarcastic sallies, had, however, the power of amusing and diverting the ever pensive and pre-occupied master of Escal-Vigor, just as the court jesters and buffoons in former days beguiled and dissipated the melancholy, or latent remorse, of tyrants. A vicious wanton, who had wallowed in the gutters of debauchery, a stable-boy from head to foot, his morals smelling as much of the dunghill as his cloth over-all and high boots, the fellow reeked of the very dregs of the populace. The cap stuck on the side of his head resembled the cap of a trooper. Ever with his hands thrust deep in his breeches' pockets, a short clay-pipe stuck in the corner of his mouth, or a quid of tobacco wandering from one cheek to the other, he would surround himself with acidulous streams of saliva, or suffocating volumes of smoke, from which his vocabulary seemed to derive its lively flavour and vivid colour.

No kindness would have touched, or softened him. As regards his master, who had picked him up out of the dirt, in spite of a shady character and deplorable references, he nourished the envy, ill-will and rancour, of a beggar against a rich man, and of a common rascal against a well-born gentleman; a ferocious angriness disguised under the devil-may-carishness of a street arab. His disinterested airs masked an unbridled hankering after trivial luxuries, for temperaments of this stamp covet those purely physical sensations exclusively, which the possession of gold can alone procure. As for the intellectual pleasures which Kehlmark enjoyed, Landrillon held them as so many frivolities.

The Count permitted a great deal of latitude to this rascal. He smiled as Landrillon rattled off his doughty deeds as a frequenter of low lodging-houses and an explorer of garrets. But, where Landrillon showed himself particularly incomparable was in his out-breaks as a woman-hater, in his paradoxical and disparaging tirades against a sex, which all the same, if he was to be believed, had never been sparing in its favors to him.

Whilst they lived in town, Landrillon was not lodged in the Dowager's house, but above the stables situated at some distance from the villa, as Madame de Kehlmark had never been able to support his monkeyish grimaces.

At present the fellow was well established in the house, and, as the soldier's saying goes, if he concealed his play he had at least well drawn up his plan. Not likely that he would be content all his life with the pickings and perquisites of an unfaithful domestic! The groom had projects of quite other importance. If rough Claudie aimed at becoming the Countess of Kehlmark, Landrillon was looking forward to espousing the housekeeper of the château. It goes without saying that he had guessed, from the first, the liaison between Henry and Blandine; but not at all ill-stomached at that, he would be well content with the leavings of his master. The manageress of Escal-Vigor was a sufficiently appetising wench in the eyes of our amateur, but he would marry her above all, for the love of the "splendid bit of spoof which she had managed to ring out of the old woman." On his side, our executioner of hearts considered he had not drawn a bad number in the lottery of personal advantages, and, moreover, he possessed into the bargain, some rather fat savings.

With all this, the honest-mannered Blandine commanded in the mind of the swaggering astonisher of trashy hussies, no small amount of respect. "Ah," he ruminated, "she has the looks of a real lady, the damsel!" No doubt of it, she'd do him credit commodiously installed behind the zinc counter of a fashionable sporting bar, that should be the resort and meeting-house of bookmakers and their dupes.

"But you must begin, my boy, by getting the individual to like you," said Landrillon to himself. So far, sharing the dislike of the late Countess, she had shown the valet scant sympathy; but Thibaut Heartsmasher was not the man to suffer himself to be easily put off. Besides, there was no hurry, he had plenty of time.

Possibly she was still cheating herself with some matrimonial illusion in the direction of Kehlmark! Thibaut was much astonished to see her, now a person of independent means, accompany Kehlmark to Smaragdis. It was that even, which decided him to go with them.

"Hang it!" said he to himself. "If she sticks with the boss, it's only because she flatters herself on being able to ensnare him. Rotten counting, all the same! The youngster seems to have taken his bellyful of her! Devil a bit of chance that he'll ever marry you, my girl!"—"But, I catch on," he ruminated another day, pulling his nose, which, with him, was a sign of satisfaction! "the sly hussy thinks to round out her money-bag by taking the management of the house. No bad taste that! We'll only hit it off together all the better."

The scoundrel reckoned up everybody else's conscience by the scale of his own. Such artful villains miss the scent entirely when it is a matter of discovering noble motives.

At Escal-Vigor he resolved to push his point without further hesitation. Neglected by the Dykgrave and feeling weary and the time tedious Mrs. Housekeeper might perhaps be more inclined to lend an ear to the declarations of the gallant coachman. If the minx should continue to entrench herself behind grand airs and to drape herself in virtue, the fellow hoped to reach his ends by other arguments; should patience and persuasion fail to win him his ends, he had quite made up his mind to take her by surprise and enjoy her by main force. Where would be the harm? Good heavens, she might have fallen in with a male much more repulsive than he! As regards personal advantages, the coachman considered himself at least the equal of his master. The fair one would thus lose nothing over the exchange.

Kehlmark continued to put up with the tone and manners of this free-mouthed jack-a-napes, as to whose real character and disposition he was completely mistaken. The Count was even minded to believe that the licentiousness and cynicism of the fellow were the result of an excess of frankness and a largeness of views, almost philosophic, and analogous some what to his own ideas.

The Count had moreover, been touched by the eagerness with which the domestic had agreed to quit the capital and accompany him to Smaragdis:

"So thou, too, wilt come and bury thyself with me on this gull's perch, my poor Thibaut? Well, that's not bad of thee!"

He was far from imagining the real springs of action in the ruffian's mind, his utter blindness even going so far as to consider his fidelity and devotion as on a par with that of the noble Blandine. In truth, he would perhaps have less easily spared the snakish, petulant presence of the valet, than the enveloping tenderness and devoted fervour of Blandine.

The reader will better understand from the sequel how it was that the raillery, perpetual sarcasms, and blasphemies of this low-minded rogue soothed the Dykgrave's embittered spirit. It will be seen too, how such an affectionate, subtle, and passionate nature tolerated so long the vicinity of this perfectly hoggish character, who was incapable of comprehending any love whatsoever, and whose experiences of sexual relationship had been, all his life, confined to the atmosphere of tripe-shops and brothels.

PART THE SECOND
THE SACRIFICES OF BLANDINE

I

The next day but one after the housewarming the Dykgrave paid a visit to the farm, "Les Pelerins." He arrived there on horseback, preceded by three dusty, barking, Gordon setters. The farmer, who was turning over a break in a neighbouring field, threw aside his spade, and had barely time to slip on his vest over his red flannel shirt; while his daughter did not take the trouble to pull down her sleeves over her arms, which were plump and red. Both ran, in a breathless state, to meet the distinguished visitor, and after a warm welcome, they set to work to do the honours of the farm.

Michael Govaertz had not unduly boasted. The whole establishment, from the dwellinghouse itself down to the smallest outhouses, the stables, stalls, cellars, barn and poultry-yard displayed order, opulence, and a rough sort of comfort.

Henry again showed himself very attentive towards Claudie, taking an interest in the management of the farm, getting explanations from the farmer's daughter, stopping with complacence and without showing the least signs of boredom, before the stores of potatoes, beetroot, beans or grain, which were shown to him in heated granaries or dark, moist outhouses. He lingered behind more than once to gaze at certain labours of the farm-hands, much admiring, for example, the action of two ploughboys, the one standing up on a cartload of clover, the other stationed at the entrance of a barn and receiving on his fork the bundles of red flowers which his companion threw to him. Of brown complexion, eyes of crockery blue, a childish smile on their thick lips displaying a sound row of teeth, they worked with a swagger, and Claudie having hailed them in a bold, guttural voice, they redoubled their sculpturesque and somewhat suggestive exertions. She encouraged them pretty much as she would have done painstaking beasts of burden.

Kehlmark inquired after the young Guidon, but in an indifferent manner, and as it were through simple politeness to the family. The scapegrace must be over there, somewhere about Klaarvatsch. Claudie pointed to the horizon at the other end of the island with a gesture of boredom, and shrugging her shoulders, hastened to change the subject.

Claudie monopolised the visitor and he seemed to have no attention but for her, no look except for what she pointed out to him. Encouraged by her example, he stroked the shining backs of the cows;

she made him taste the foaming milk with which the sturdy milkmaids were filling brown earthenware jars. In a neighbouring apartment other amazons were churning butter. The insipid savour disgusted Henry, who preferred to breathe the strong-smelling atmosphere of the stable, where his horse was engaged in chewing fresh clover, in company with the robust palfreys of the farm. In the garden she gathered for him a bouquet of lilacs and pinks, which she herself placed, not without handling him somewhat, in the opening of his waistcoat. "You must come again in the strawberry season," she said, stooping down, on the pretext of showing him some ripening berries, but in reality to inflame him by the enticing contour and flexions of her full-fleshed frame.

"Already noon!" exclaimed Kehlmark, drawing out his watch as the hour sounded from the steeple of the Zoudbertinge church.

The farmer invited him, with a laugh, to share their country soup, but without venturing to hope that he would accept.

"Willingly," he said, "but on condition of eating at the servants' table, and even of dipping in the dish like them."

"What an idea!" exclaimed Claudie, flattered however, by this want of ceremony. This condescension even seemed to her of a nature to reduce the distance between this very urbane gentleman and a simple daughter of the soil.

"All these people here burst with health!" declared Kehlmark, including the whole table in one look around. "They are as nice as what they are devouring, and their appetising air adds to the flavour of the dish."

Following the country custom, the women served the men and did not eat till the latter had finished. They provided a sort of pottage of bacon and vegetables into which Henry was the first to dip his tin spoon. His two neighbours, the labourers who had been warehousing the clover, followed his example with alacrity.

"And does not your son return to dinner?" inquired Kehlmark of the burgomaster.

"Oh, as for him, he takes his bread and meat with him every morning," was the reply of Claudie.

After dinner, Henry seemed in no hurry to go; Claudie, convinced that this was owing to her charms, still walked him up and down the Govaertz lands. She cleverly enlightened him as to their fortune. Their fields extended so far, in that direction, beyond the windmill. "There, where you see that white birch." She gave the Dykgrave to understand that they were very rich already, quite apart from their expectations. Michael's two sisters, the two old bigots, although they had quarrelled with the Burgomaster, had promised to leave their fortune to his children.

Kehlmark had allowed time to drag on so that it was evening when it occurred to him to call for his horse. The Count was hoping to see the little bugler again, and at the moment of making up his mind to depart, he made another inquiry after him. "Often he does not return till night," said Claudie, scowling at the mere mention of the despised urchin. "He sometimes even sleeps outside. His vagabond ways no longer trouble my father or me. Besides, we are not surprised."

With a contraction at the heart the Count thought of the poor lad, benighted in a disreputable district.

"By-the-bye, Burgomaster," he said just as the farmer brought him his horse, "I wish to be one of your Musical Society."

"Do better, Count, be our president and protector." "Agreed, I accept."

Thinking of Guidon, the Count had remembered the serenade of the night before last, and said to himself that it would be sweet to hear often that simple, melancholy air which the young shepherd played so well.

With one foot in the stirrup another idea occurred to him; something stuck in his heart. Was he to go away without approaching the real object of his visit?

"It is possible," he decided to say timidly to the farmer, "that your son has serious inclinations for music and drawing. Send him to me. Perhaps there may be a means of making something of him. I will try to civilise the little savage."

"Monsieur is too good," stammered Govaertz, "but frankly I am afraid you will lose your pains. The scapegrace will do you no credit."

"On the contrary, Monsieur," added the lad's sister, "he will only be an occasion to you of annoyance. He does not care for anybody or anything; or rather, he has eccentric tastes and proclivities, thinking black when honest people think white."

"Never mind, I will try the experiment," resumed the Count of Kehlmark, striking the dust off his boots with his whip, and putting as little expression as possible into his voice. "I confess I have a liking for difficult tasks, for those that require perseverance and even some courage. Thus, I have tamed and brought into good order restive horses. I even admit, and this is not to my credit, that it sometimes suffices to induce me to undertake a task if you defy me to do it. Difficulty excites and danger intoxicates me. I have the gambler's mania. By entrusting to me this wrongheaded, undisciplined youth, you would oblige me. Let me see! It is possible," he added, "I may go and take up the young fellow tomorrow, as I shall be riding in the neighbourhood of Klaarvatsch. I will talk with him and take his measure."

"As you will, Count," said Claudie. "In any case it is doing us much honour. We shall even be grateful to you on his account. But do not blame us if the ne'er-do-well does not improve under your care and advice."

The next day the Dykgrave rode as far as the Klaarvatsch heaths. He soon noticed the little chap in the midst of a group of ragged urchins, squatting around a fire of twigs and roots, upon which they were frying potatoes. At the approach of the horseman they all stood up, and with the exception of Guidon, ran away scared, to hide in the bushes. The young Govaertz, making a visor of his hand, looked boldly at the Count of Kehlmark.

"Ah, it is thee, boy," said Kehlmark, "Come here, wilt thou, and hold my horse a moment, while I arrange my stirrups."

The young fellow approached with confidence and took the reins. All the time he was shortening the straps, an operation which served Henry merely as a pretext, to gain time to put a face upon the matter, he observed him from the corner of his eye, not knowing how to commence the conversation, while the youngster on his side did not lose one of his movements, and felt himself strangely troubled, at once dreading and wishing for what was about to pass between them. Their eyes met and seemed to put to one another a poignant and subtle question. Then Kehlmark, in order to finish the matter, went up to the boy, took him by the hand, and gazing into the depth of his eyes, repeated to him, not without hesitation, the offer which he had made the night before to the boy's family.

"Thou understandest! Thou'lt come every day to the chateau. I will teach thee myself to read and write, to draw and to paint, to make fine, big pictures such as those thou didst admire the other evening. And we will also go in for music, plenty of music! Thou wilt see! We shall not tire one another."

The boy listened to him without saying a word, so dazed that he had a stupefied air, with disparted lips, his eyes wide open and staring, looked almost haggard. The Count stopped short, taken aback, thinking he must have adopted the wrong way, but continued to search his face. All at once, Guidon changed colour, his visage contracted, and he broke into a nervous laugh. At the same time, to the profound emotion of Kehlmark, he drew back, and attempted to withdraw his hand from the Count's; one would have thought he was resisting and wished to rejoin his young companions who were much amused at this scene. The Count, discouraged, let him go.

The little savage darted towards the other cowboys, but then stopped short, ceased laughing, put both his hands before his eyes, and let himself fall down on the grass where he wallowed, his body shaken by sobs, biting at the heather and knocking his naked feet together.

The Count, more and more discomposed, ran to pick him up:

"For heaven's sake, dear boy, calm thyself! Thou hast not understood me. Thou'rt wrong to be alarmed. I will never forgive myself for having hurt thee. On the contrary, I wish to do thee good. I flattered myself to deserve thy confidence, to become thy great friend. And thou gettest into this painful state! Let us suppose I have said nothing. Be at ease! I will not take thee away against thy will. Farewell!"

And the Count was about to leap into his saddle. But the young Govaertz half stood up, dragged himself on his knees to the Count, seized his hands, embraced them, bedewed them with his tears, and at last burst out, relieving himself of a torrent of exclamatory words, as though, held in check for so long, he had at last succeeded in bursting free:—

"Oh, Monsieur, pardon! I am mad! I do not know what happens to me, what is going on within me; I have the appearance of being sad, but I am too happy; I seemed to die of joy in hearing you! If I weep it is because you are too good. And then at first, I could scarcely believe. You are not making a jest, are you ? It is really true you will take me to your house?"

The Dykgrave, attracted as he was by this impressionable little peasant, had never expected to encounter such an affectionate nature. He gently familiarised him with the idea of the happiness, which was in store for him, and ended by leaving him in a state of rapture, his face illuminated with joy, after having appointed a meeting for the very next day at Escal-Vigor.

II

After this understanding, Guidon came every day to the chateau. Kehlmark shut himself up with him for long hours in his studio. The young peasant applied himself to learning, endeavouring with a neophyte's zeal and ardour, worthy of a *creato* or apprentice of the masters of the Italian Renaissance. No recreation for either was comparable to this initiation. Guidon was at once the model, the pupil, and the disciple of Kehlmark. When they were tired of writing, reading or drawing, Guidon would take his bugle, or maybe, with his bell-like voice he would sing heroic airs of ancient times, which he had learned from the Klaarvatsch fishermen.

Kehlmark could no longer do without his pupil and had him sent for, if he delayed to come. The one was never seen without the other. They had become inseparable. Guidon usually dined at Escal-Vigor, so that he hardly ever returned to Les Pelerins except to sleep. As Guidon improved, and developed exceptional gifts, Kehlmark's intense affection for his pupil became exclusive, even suspicious and almost selfish. Henry reserved to himself the privilege of being the only one to form this character, to enjoy this admirable nature, which should be his finest work, and to breathe the air of this delicate spirit. He cultivated the boy's mind jealously, like those rabid horticulturists who would murder the indiscreet intruder or the designing competitor, who might venture into their domains. There was a gentle intimacy between them. They sufficed the one to the other. The amazed Guidon dreamed of no other paradise than Escal-Vigor. Fame, or the desire of applause, never disturbed their life of pure artists.

Kehlmark had seen pretty closely the social and external life of self-styled artists. He knew the vanity of reputations, the prostitution of glory, the iniquity of success, the impurity of criticism, the competition among rivals of a nature more fierce and abominable than that between sordid shopkeepers.

Blandine, although a little distrustful, had cordially welcomed this guest to the château. Happy at the felicity which the young Govaertz procured for Henry, she received him kindly, without always succeeding in showing much enthusiasm. Indeed, without feeling an absolute antipathy to this little peasant, she must have been sometimes wounded to the quick, hurt to the very marrow, and notwithstanding her good heart, her sound reason and her greatness of soul, she had no doubt frequent movements of impatience against this intimate, intellectual commerce, this close comradeship, this perfect understanding between the two men. She even went so far as to be jealous of the talent and temperament, of the spiritual gifts which brought the young artist nearer to Kehlmark's soul than all the love of her, a simple woman, guardian of his happiness. The good creature showed nothing of these moments, so human in their weakness, but, for which her reason reproached her instinct.

As for Claudie, she was not at the outset, nor even for some time later, offended by the favour which the Dykgrave showed the young Govaertz. She saw in it a way the Count had of paying court indirectly to the sister, by patronising the brother. No doubt, Kehlmark would make the young shepherd the confidant of his love for the young farm-mistress. "He is too timid to declare himself directly to me," she said to herself, "he will open his mind at first to the youngster and will endeavour to learn from him the nature of my sentiments. He has chosen a rather sorry go-between. But he had no choice. Meanwhile, the solicitude that the Count shows the wicked rascal is meant rather for myself." And quite infatuated, the rough girl rejoiced at this perpetual intimacy of the Dykgrave with the scapegrace so long repudiated, almost denied by his relatives. She even came to soften the roughness and harshness of her behaviour towards her younger brother. She now cherished him, surrounded him with attentions, took trouble with his clothes, looked after his linen; to none of which luxuries had he ever before been accustomed. In order to explain this change of conduct, Claudie had taken Govaertz into her confidence as to her great matrimonial project. The Burgomaster, no less ambitious, applauded these lofty views, nor did he, for an instant, doubt of success. Following the example of his favourite child, he ceased to be rough with his boy and became more considerate towards him.

When, after a few months of so-called trial, the Dykgrave declared to the Burgomaster that he would definitely take upon himself the care of the pretended good-for-nothing, Claudie induced Michael Govaertz to accept this proposal.

The Burgomaster, who was very vain, had somewhat hesitated, because so far as he understood, the situation "of Guidon at the chateau would be that of an underling, or a valet, a little superior to Landrillon, but a valet all the same.

Although, when so long under his own roof, he had degraded his son, giving him the lowest place in his gang of labourers and leaving to him the dirtiest farm work, his paternal vanity would have suffered, to see him dependent on any other authority than his own. To justify his intervention, Kehlmark had submitted to the Govaertzes drawings, already very meritorious, of the young apprentice, but the father was no more capable than the daughter of understanding the promise contained in these first attempts.

"Let us accept the Dykgrave's offers," insisted Claudie, meeting her father's objections. "In the first place, it is a good riddance for us. Then, you may be sure the Count would not burden himself with this scapegrace nor invite him at all, but to be agreeable to us, and to testify his interest in me. We should be disobliging him, believe me, to frustrate his good intentions. It's his mode of opening to me the doors of Escal-Vigor. Between ourselves, he doubtless thinks nothing of this dauber, or at least, exaggerates his slight merits."

In the early days, when Guidon returned in the evening from the château, she would question him as to how they had spent the time, how things went on at Escal-Vigor, and upon the words and manner of the Dykgrave. "Did the Count inquire after me? What did he say to thee? He has a great interest in us, has he not? Go on, let us hear; speak out, conceal nothing from me. Certainly he must have confessed to thee a certain weakness for thy sister?"

Guidon replied evasively, but so as not to compromise himself. Yes, the Count for sure had inquired after her, as also after their father and even the servants; why, yes even of the farm beasts, too. But not with great anxiety. The fact was, Claudie had played a very small part in the conversations of the master and the disciple, who were entirely taken up with their studies and occupations.

Guidon became more and more discreet. From their first association he had vowed to his protector a fidelity as complete and as intense as Blandine's. To her fanatical affection he joined that something of acuteness and lucidity, which intelligence and brain-culture add to sentiment. Guidon, the so-called stupid, the simpleton, the rustic good-for-nothing, represented moral value, in a body which was of an admirable form and which daily increased in strength and beauty.

With the tact, the second-sight, the instinct of loving natures, he suspected his sister's foolish infatuation for the Dykgrave, but he foresaw also that the Count would never return her affection. Guidon was but too well acquainted with his sister Claudie, and he knew better than anyone the abysses of vulgarity and the absolute incompatibilities existing between her and Kehlmark.

The pupil had even reached the point of perceiving that he was preferred by his master to "Madame the Housekeeper," the noble Blandine. It is certain that the Count always seemed more taken up with him than with the woman who loved him. Guidon was inwardly proud of the predilection of which he was the object, and by his attentions to the young woman, it might have been supposed that he wished to win her pardon for the excessive part which he played in the master's life.

Guidon guessed and felt rightly: Henry never revealed himself or opened his mind freely except to his disciple. With others he kept himself reserved, nor did his kindly words assume the caressing tone, the unction and smoothness, which characterised his outpourings to his favourite boy.

Blandine had never seen him so gay and radiant as since the time he had undertaken the education and charged himself with the destiny of this young ragamuffin. However much deference and devotion the lad showed towards the lady, he was unable to disguise his joy at having become the principal and constant care of the master of Escal-Vigor. He showed no malice, only a simple joy; nay, he even grew tender with regard to the almost forsaken woman, and with the egotism of a spoiled child or chosen neophyte, he did not notice the silence and reserve of Blandine when the Count kept him to dinner, nor the strange looks which she darted at both of them when they conversed with warmth and excitement, rapt in a common lyric feeling and regardless of the presence of the witness.

The Zoudbertinge villagers did not, for an instant, look with jealous eyes at the special favour the Dykgrave accorded to the son of Govaertz.

As little as the Burgomaster and his daughter did they believe in the talent and the vocation of the youth.

"It's a real kindness and a charity," said they among themselves. "His father would not have known what to do with this wild and intractable young trifler, who used to despise the work as much as the amusements of the apprentices of his age."

The clowns even wondered that the Count had succeeded in getting the semblance of any work whatever out of the youth, who had learned nothing up to then, except to play tolerably well on the bugle.

Moreover, the dearer the master and pupil became to each other the more did Kehlmark show himself gracious, liberal, and even profuse, making generous presents to the tuneful brotherhoods and multiplying occasions of festivities and athletic tourneys.

He instituted regattas with sailing-vessels round the island, in which seated with Guidon in a yacht adorned with his colours, he almost surpassed the best sailors of the country. He renewed at his own expense the musical instruments of the St. Cecilia guild, was constantly present at the rehearsals, the excursions, and the festivities of this group of young fellows, and it even happened more than once on the fine summer nights, when the twilight and the dawn seem almost to embrace, after a long evening made up of athletic interludes and brisk bouts of buffoonery, that he would lead all the band in a tramp across the island, and not restore the riotous roysterers to their conjugal or paternal firesides till the following evening, after a picturesque caravaning enlivened with leaping, belly-fillings, guzzlings, and exploits of gallantry among the stubble and the hay.

Kehlmark spent his money without reckoning. One might have supposed that he sought by excessive liberality and indiscriminate charity to purchase his right to a mysterious and forbidden happiness; that he wished in some sort to pay the ransom of a jealous and frail felicity.

These mad largesses no doubt increased Blandine's anxiety; however, she did not risk any remonstrance, but devised how she might best meet these ill-considered expenses.

Of course, there was in the popularity of the Dykgrave a good deal of false worship, baseness, and cupidity, but if most of the rustics loved him in a coarse manner, at least they loved him after their fashion. The poor devils of fellows of Klaarvatsch especially would have let themselves be chopped in pieces for their young lord.

As for declared enemies, the Count knew of none, save the minister, Balthus Bomberg and a few mock-modest bigots. Every Sunday the minister thundered against the impiety and the shamelessness of the Dykgrave and threatened with hell the sheep who followed this libertine, this ravening wolf; he mourned especially the over venturesome visitors who frequented Escal-Vigor, that diabolical château decorated with scandalous nudities.

Although at daggers-drawn with the Burgomaster, this bilious little man, in his narrow, fanatical zeal, decided to pay a visit to Les Pelerins, in order to point out to the father the risk he was running in entrusting the education of the young Govaertz to this wicked rich man, who was scandalising the community with his concubinage and impiety. Like all inveterate Calvinists, Balthus was also an iconoclast. Had he not feared the fury of the peasants, so attached to the old relics, which reminded them of the stubborness of their ancestors, he would have had the fine fresco of the *Martyrdom of St. Olfgar* scraped out.

Kehlmark was doubly odious to him, as pagan and as artist. In order to intimidate the Burgomaster, Balthus called on him to tear his son away from the patron who was corrupting him, on pain of causing both his children, Claudie and Guidon, to be disinherited by their venerable aunts. Michael and Claudie, more and more taken with their Dykgrave, packed the troublesome man off to his church with abundance of sarcasm and mockery. Guidon, whom he accosted one day in the neighbourhood of Escal-Vigor park, would not even listen to him, but turned his back on him with a shrug of the shoulders and a still grosser gesture.

However, Claudie's business did not seem to advance sensibly. "See here, thou doesn't tell me anything, sleepy head!" said she to him, whom she imagined to be the connecting link between herself and Kehlmark. "Has not the Count entrusted thee with a special message for me?" Guidon would invent some fiction, but often taken off his guard, he would give himself away or keep his mouth closed. The coarse-grained faggot then flew into a rage at her go-between's stupidity, and it itched her to cuff and brutalize him as in former days.

Through policy the Dykgrave continued his visits to Les Pelerins and his attentions to the young farm-girl. She would have wished him more enterprising. He took a good deal of time to make up his mind to propose: he had hardly ventured to trifle with the tips of her fingers and never had he stolen a kiss!

No sooner did she hear the trotting of his horse and the yelping of his escort of setters, Claudie would run to the farm-door, almost taking pleasure in thus publicly advertising her love, so certain was she of success. Accordingly, people began to talk a good deal, in the evenings, of the Dykgrave's attentions to her.

Although his affections were monopolised almost exclusively by young Guidon, the Dykgrave aimed at being favourably regarded by everybody. He even pushed magnanimity so far as to endeavour to conciliate the minister. In reply to the denunciations and anathemas of the virulent pastor, he scattered alms freely, ruining himself with gifts of clothing and food for the poor directly dependent on the parish. The minister distributed the money and the other offerings, but was by no means disarmed thereby.

More than once, Henry's friends, the shrimp fishermen and the vagabonds of the Klaarvatsch beach, offered to bring the minister to reason; especially five of them, who were permanently employed at the chateau and formed a sort of bodyguard to Kehlmark. Grandsons of old-time wreckers, casual dikemen, plunderers of jetsam—the painter often made them pose and amused himself with their wrestling and their knife-play deadened-edged, or perhaps, he would confess them, enjoying with Guidon their rough language and the coarse-mouthed stories of their prowesses. These hulking big chaps, incorrigible skulkers, who had never been able anywhere to acclimatise themselves and had got themselves everywhere dismissed, these splendid sprigs of humanity, the first masters of young Guidon, now swore only by Henry and Escal-Vigor.

"Just say the word," suggested now one, now another, to Kehlmark. "Would you like us to sack the parsonage, or hang up high and dry this canting psalm-singer; or rather, should we skin him clean as the Smaragdites once did the apostle Olfgar, that other spoil-sport?"

And they would certainly have done as they said, at a word, or a gesture from their master, and with them, all would have let themselves loose on the importunate preacher.

Several times, in passing by the parsonage, the musicians of the guild of St. Cecilia loudly hooted. One evening after deep potations they even went so far as to break the windows. On St. Sylvester's day they placed against the minister's door a frightful manikin of straw with a head of brown bread, representing his most faithful companion and second self Mrs. Bömberg; and as, in consequence of this insult, he broke out into fresh invectives against the Dykgrave and Blandine, the Klaarvatsch rascals splashed with excrement the front of the parsonage, which had just been re-painted.

Jaundiced with spite and rancour, the pastor seemed to stand alone against the whole parish and even against the entire island.

"How," Balthus Bomberg asked himself, "how reduce this haughty Kehlmark? How undermine his prestige, detach from him these misled and blinded brutes, and make them rise against their idol and burn what they adore?"

Far from listening to him they deserted his church. In the end, he preached but to empty benches. A dozen bigoted old women, including his wife and the two sisters of the Burgomaster alone remained to support him.

In the idolatrous devotion which the young Dykgrave had excited there was mingled something of the worship which the Roman populace had for Nero, their indulgent and prodigal provider of bread and games.

III

While lavishing his attentions on those around him and on the community in general, Kehlmark redoubled his marks of kindness to Landrillon. He treated him with more good humour than ever, affecting to take fresh pleasure in his barrack-room yarns.

But the rascal was not the dupe of this manifestation of good-will. Without showing aught thereof, he had not delayed to take umbrage at the influence of the little Guidon Govaertz on Henry de Kehlmark, and perhaps he surprised a slight glimpse—nothing renders us more perspicacious than envy—of the extent of the affection which these two beings bore to one another. Let the reader imagine the feeling of ignoble jealousy that might affect a circus clown who sees success and popularity abandon him for the sake of a comedian of graver and more serious cast, and he will understand the deep, long-contained ill-will that the coachman nourished for the little peasant. Kehlmark almost always took Govaertz with him in his drives, and it was Landrillon who drove them. On an excursion which they made to Upperzyde to visit the museum and have another look at the Franz Hals, the young Govaertz shared the apartment of his master, while Landrillon was relegated to the garret under the roof. Worse still, the servant was forced to serve this ragamuffin at table—this ne'er-do-well, formerly the laughing-stock and scapegoat of the Smaragdis labourers, and now swollen with importance, cherished, petted, and become the inseparable companion of Monsieur. To think that this great lord seemed unable to dispense with the company of this wretched young errand-runner, who spoiled his fine paper, expensive canvas, and costly paints!

Had not the varlet dreamed of becoming the husband of Blandine, he would, perhaps, have been even worse disposed towards the cursed shepherd lad. Up to a certain point, the servant was not displeased at the exclusive importance which the young Govaertz was assuming in the life of the Count. Landrillon looked forward to making a good use at the proper time of this intimacy between the two men, in order to detach Blandine from her master. Neglected and even abandoned by Kehlmark, the poor woman would naturally be more inclined to listen to a new gallant.

Availing himself of a moment when Blandine had gone into the kitchen to attend to some household matter, Landrillon ventured one day to make his declaration:—

"I have some small savings," he hasarded, "and if it is true that the old lady left you a portion of her stored-up "spoof" we shall make a nice couple, do you not think so, Mam'zelle Blandine? For while you are a pretty enough mouthful you must allow there are uglier fellows than me. Lots of fine wenches of your sex have, for the rest, found out ways to convince me of it," added the would-be seducer, twirling his mustache. Much disgusted with this declaration, Blandine declined coldly and with dignity the honour which he offered her, without taking the trouble to give the least reason for her refusal.

"Eh, what, Mam'zelle! that can't be your *last* word. You'll consider. Boasting apart, marriers of my stamp, gallants with none but good intentions, are not come across every day."

"Do not insist, Monsieur Landrillon; I have only one answer." "Ah, then, you must have designs on someone else."

"No, I shall never marry."

"Well, then at least you love somebody else?"

"That must be my secret and a matter between my conscience and myself."

Rather elevated, for he had drunk several glasses of gin in order to give himself a little Dutch courage, he ventured to take her by the waist, squeeze her, and even steal a kiss. But she pushed him away, and as he began again, fetched him a box of the ears, threatening to complain to the Count. So, for the time, he considered he had said enough.

This scene took place in the early days of their settling down at Escal-Vigor.

But Landrillon did not consider himself beaten. He returned to the charge, taking advantage of moments when he found himself alone with her, to importune her with familiarities and liberties.

Whenever he had been drinking she ran serious danger. What times the Count retired to his studio with Guidon or they went out together, Landrillon seized the opportunity to harass the young woman. He pursued her from one apartment to another, and to escape from his enterprise, she had to shut herself up in her room, although he went so far as to threaten to break in the door.

Just as in the town, in the days of the Dowager, Henry had no one to serve him in the house except Blandine and Landrillon. The five Klaarvatsch lads attached to his person were not housed in the château.

So that very often, the unfortunate housekeeper found herself almost abandoned to the mercy of this rascal.

Life became unbearable to the young woman. If she refrained from complaining to Kehlmark, it was because she thought this trifling joker, this low bred buffoon, was indispensable to Henry's amusement. Such was her devotion to the Dykgrave that the noble girl would have scrupled to deprive him of the least object capable of diverting him from his melancholy and depression. Thus she witnessed with a stoical self-denial the influence which the young Govaertz was obtaining over the mind of her master, and she even endeavoured to smile graciously on her lover's favourite.

She therefore endured the teasing and importunity of the satyr and contented herself with escaping as well as she could from his violence.

Blandine's resistance and contempt only exasperated the ruffian's desire. One day he was even on the point of forcing his odious passion on to her by brute strength, when she armed herself with a kitchen knife, left lying on the table, and threatened to plunge it into his belly.

Then, as he drew back, she fled in tears towards the staircase, determined to go up to the Count's room and denounce to him the rascal's disgraceful conduct.

"As thou wilt," sneered Landrillon, pale with rage and lust, and likewise resolved to go to extremities. "But in thy place, I'd do nothing of the sort. I don't fancy thou'lt be quite welcome up there. He's more likely to be cross with thee for disturbing him. For if thou hast still a fondness for him, he don't care a brass button for thee, thy quondam lover!"

"What do you mean?" protested the young woman, stopping on the first step.

"Oh, it's no use playing the innocent! We know what we know, hang it all! Thou hast been his mistress, don't deny it."

"Landrillon!"

"Ay, it is the gossip of Zoudbertinge and even of all Smaragdis. The Rev. Balthus Bomberg never ceases to thunder against 'the Dykgrave's street-walker'."

Giving up her intention of ascending the stairs, she retraced her steps, let herself sink into a chair, fainting, and almost lifeless with grief and shame.

A prelude on the piano broke the silence which they both kept.

Guidon was singing up there, with his rustic voice, (just broken and still a little defective, but of singularly magnetic power), a wrecker's ballad, which Kehlmark accompanied on the piano.

Her body shaken with sobs, that seemed to keep time, Blandine, grief-struck, listened to the measure of the song; the young fellow's voice seemed to put the crowning touch to her woe.

An equivocal smile curled the lips of the valet as he heard the song, and he regarded unhappy Blandine with a no less ironical look.

"See here," he said, in a wheedling tone, touching her on the shoulder, "don't let us fall out with each other my fine one. Listen to me rather. Its only your good that's wanted, confound it all! You'd be nice and wrong to keep on loving this neglectful and disdainful aristo. What a deceiver! Don't you see he has ceased to care for you?"

And as she raised her head he made her a sign, putting his finger to his mouth, to listen to the strangely passionate song which the disciple was singing to his master, and after another silence, during which they both lent their ears to the sounds from above, he said in a low voice:—

"You see, our master thinks much more of this peasant boy than of you or me. Therefore, in your place, I'd leave him in the lurch and let him give himself up to this blackguard and the other brutes of peasants. Here, Blandine, you will wear yourself out with sorrow, you'll fade away through vexation. Your beauty will vanish without being of advantage to the least creature on God's earth. If you'll take my advice, my dear, we will both return to the town. I have had enough of our holiday at Smaragdis. It is not to be believed, but since this sly young wretch entered the château there's nothing for anybody but him! You and I sink into the background. What a sudden infatuation! Two fingers of the same hand are not more inseparable."

"Well, what can you have to object to this attachment?" said Blandine, seeking once more to overcome her misgivings. "This Guidon Govaertz is a nice boy, unappreciated by his relatives, much superior, as everything shows, by his intelligence and sentiments, to the most part of these coarse islanders. The Count is right to make so much of the poor child, who for the rest, grows every day more and more deserving of his kindnesses."

"Yes, agreed; but Monsieur exaggerates his patronage. He does not sufficiently observe a proper distance, but shows, really, too much affection for the snotty nose. A Count of Kehlmark should not mix himself up too much, hang it! with a former cow and swine herdsman."

"Once more, what do you mean?"

For reply, Landrillon merely plunged his hands into his pockets and, staring in the air, began to whistle a sort of parody of the little shepherd boy's song. Then he went away, reckoning he had said enough for the moment.

Left to herself, Blandine commenced again to weep. Without thinking of evil, whatever she might do to reason herself out of it, she was troubled at the perpetual companionship of the Count and his favourite. In vain she argued with herself and endeavoured to rejoice at the change in Kehlmark, his activity, his joy in life: she regretted that this moral cure was not her own work, but a miracle wrought by this youthful intruder.

"What now!" said Landrillon a few days later to the young woman, "he's *all* right, our governor is, Mam'zelle Blandine! Ah! they get on better and better, our artist chaps! Yesterday, they pecked at each other with their little beaks, how lik'st that!"

"Thou talk'st nonsense, Landrillon," she replied, laughing with an effort. "Once more, I tell you, the Count is attached to this little peasant because he does credit to his lessons. Where is the harm? I have already told thee he loves this young Govaertz like a younger brother, as an intelligent pupil whose mind he has opened and cultivated."

Landrillon hummed a light air, making an ugly grimace that was chock-full of hidden meaning.

Vicious to the marrow, having passed through the worst promiscuities of the barracks, his character was a compound of police-spy, male-prostitute, and blackmailer. Incapable of understanding anything deep or noble in ordinary affections, still less could he recognize and admit the possibility of an absolutely noble and elevated love of man for man.

As Blandine kept silent, not understanding these insinuations, he pursued "I have my own notion, Mam'zelle. My opinion is that he no longer pays much attention to petticoats, our governor, even supposing that he ever troubled about them. But, you ought to know something about it, eh? Would he have already "unharnessed," and he a young man still?"

"Landrillon!" protested Blandine, "pray refrain from such reflections. It is not for you to judge the Count. What he does is well done, do you hear?"

"Beg pardon, Mademoiselle, I'll keep quiet, perfectly quiet! But all the same, he's very mysterious, our master! He leads a strange kind of life. Always with his peasants, and especially with this little wheedler. We count for no more in his eyes than his horses and dogs. Really, I admire your indulgence for his larkings. You know better than I that he has entirely thrown you over. If it's change he requires—bless me, I also like to taste different fruits! he'd only have to look around him and choose. The prettiest girls of Smaragdis, from Zoudbertinge to Klaarvatsch would be at his disposal. I know one of them," (and he said these words not without spite, for he had already tried the ground on his own account in that quarter) "who burns to her blood and marrow to see him—how shall I say?—in her private apartment. Why it's precisely big Claudie, the very sister of the young cockswain. Although he shows himself several times a week at Les Pelerins, no one will get out of my head that the gallant is fonder of the brother's breeches than the petticoats of the sister!"

"Once more, I say, be quiet," exclaimed Blandine, her heart tightening at the idea of the love which the virago felt for Kehlmark; and knowing herself detested by the gawky thing, to such an extent that the latter did not salute her when they met each other in the lanes. As for Kehlmark's affection for Guidon, if she suffered from it involuntarily, she persisted in suspecting in it nothing abnormal or improper.

"Well, *qui vivra verra!* Mam'zelle Blandine. An occasion will soon arise to enlighten you as to the colour of the *liaison* between these two painters!" sneered Thibaut, delighted at his witty sally.

"Enough. Not another word!" cried Blandine. "I hardly know what prevents me from letting the Count know on the spot, of your abominable imputations—or rather, I know too well; for I would die of shame before daring to repeat to him what you have just said to me!"

IV

O ne evening, seated upon a bank of the dyke commanding a view of the country, Henry de Kehlmark and Guidon Govaertz, their hands joined, were pursuing one of their ineffable conversations, interrupted by silences as eloquent and fervid as their words.

It was one of those late autumn evenings favourable to the evocation of legends, in a landscape of heather in flower and under a sky of shifting clouds, the one riding astride the other. In the distance towards Klaarvatsch, beyond the park trees, our friends' view embraced an immense stretch of verdure of the colour of winelees, to which the setting sun added a further lustre. Heaps of dry wood crackled here and there; and a scent of burning wood floated in the damp atmosphere. The weather was extremely mild and the evening air exhaled a sort of languor; the breeze seemed like a labourer's panting, or the heaving of a lover consumed with desire.

At the sight of a ruddy cloud of fantastic shape, the friends remembered the story of the Fire Shepherd celebrated in all the plains of the North. Kehlmark kept silence for some time, he seemed to be revolving some serious idea in connection with these terrifying beliefs. Since he had known him, the young Govaertz had never seen him with so gloomy, sorrow-stricken an aspect.

"You are suffering, master?" he said.

"No, dear boy; an unpleasant recollection; it will pass. This evening perhaps, the air is extremely heady; dost thou not find it so? Dost know the real story of the Fire Shepherd, whereof thou spakest just now. I have every reason to believe that it is wrongly told. I think I can suggest a more correct version. I have gathered their story from these haunted landscapes on evenings like this, especially those bits of heather where melancholy used to reign even more gloomily than elsewhere, where plain and horizon distilled the essences of their heavy sadness and shady sleep. Certain details of the landscape contract, as thou wilt have noticed in keeping thy sheep, a poignant and almost prophetic significance. Nature seems to suffer from remorse. The clouds stop and accumulate in a funeral procession over a pool predestined to be the scene of a death by drowning, a crime, or a suicide.

"Dear boy, how many good resolutions have suffered shipwreck in such weather! It is better then to conjure away one's own danger

GEORGES EEKHOUD

by thinking of the misfortunes of others. I have come at last to compassionate the awful lot of even accursed Cain. It is he whom I pity and not his victims. I find him superb and attractive although sinister.

But I am talking nonsense and telling thee frightful stories like unto those old wives tell at evening tide."

"No, no; do continue; you tell a story so well, and you put so much meaning into ordinary words; your language often draws tears from me."

"Be it so. The hour is propitious. And since we are so well together here, I long to tell thee to what a degree I share the distress of the burning shepherd. For a long time he has haunted to the point of obsession the violet, nocturnal heather of my soul. I find myself, to my surprise, wandering in spirit by his side, among his sulphurous sheep, under the motions of his crook reddened in hell-fire, bitten at the heels by his black and red dog, resembling a half-burnt brand, a brand from the eternal furnace, the dog which shares his master's fate, and the half of whose body begins to burn again when the other half has resumed the appearance of life.

"This is what these phantoms have confided to me:—

Long, long ago Gerard was the shepherd of a couple of old and miserly peasants, living in a remote and isolated spot, full of steppes and deserts, like those down there at Klaarvatsch. No one knew from whence he came. When he was discovered for the first time he might have been fifteen years of age; he ran about half dressed; his appearance was like that of a wild animal and it was necessary to teach him to speak, like a child. At a venture, the old misers had him baptised, and taking him into their service brought him up to guard their sheep. He only cost them his pittance which was worse than frugal, and by taking him they had the credit of doing a good action.

"Doubtless mother Nature cherished this wild lad, for engendered by, one knows not what, woodland creatures, and repudiated by men, he seemed never to grow older, but became ever stronger and handsomer. He was a tall youth, and so well provided with hair that stray locks kept falling on his forehead and on his lovely eyes, wherein the infinite depths of eternity seem to lay.

"It was labour in vain to catechise him; he never attached much importance to our narrow rites and mummeries. In simple nature he found his model and his counsellor. In other words, he followed nothing but his instincts.

"However, after a long time, his master and mistress, although advanced in years, had a child, quite a delicate little boy, to whom they gave the name of Stephen. As the parents were too old to attend to him, it was Gerard who brought him up. The young man began by choosing for him two of his favourite sheep as nurses. Stephen shot up and became a chubby child, rosy and pretty as an angel. Gerard continued to keep for him the best milk of his sheep, the sweetest fruits, and the eggs of ringdoves and pheasants. He adored him as no other human being ever adored another, his poor wild heart having never been able to expend the treasures of affection which it had accumulated. Stephen chirped like a bird; he was as fair as the other was dark; and the little fellow ordered about the big, wild boy. The old couple, selfish and crotchety to the point of mania, let them wander about together and live as they would.

"When they bathed in the Démer, Gerard admired this youthful frame, so slender and graceful, and knew no pleasure comparable to that of embracing the boy's warm and supple body, carrying him in his arms a long time and very far, deep into the midst of the woods, where they would finally roll about amongst the ferns and mosses. Gerard would tickle Stephen by passing his lips over his rosy skin. And the child would laugh, would attempt to escape, kicking out with his tiny feet, or else would bestow hearty slaps on the robust hinderparts of the big boy, who took these blows as so many caresses.

"This idyll lasted till the day when Stephen's parents received a visit from two cousins, accompanied by Wanna, a fair young girl of Stephen's age, brisk and lively as a clear frosty dawn, and as tasty as a woodland strawberry. The old people on both sides agreed to marry the children, who were pleased with each other at first sight.

"From the arrival of Wanna, Gerard became quite sad on account of the attention which the little Stephen bestowed on his nice cousin. Stephen was a spoiled child, who only loved Gerard as he might have loved a docile and faithful dog, the partner of his play, the humourer of all his whims. Gerard looked on Wanna with sombre, almost murderous eyes; but the fair lass did but laugh at the savage, and to annoy him, being of sportive and crafty humour, she would often carry off Stephen, or run away and hide herself so that he might come and rejoin her far from the jealous youth.

"Gerard, at the end of his patience, implored his friend not to marry. Stephen laughed in his face. "Art thou crazy, dearest fellow? Its nature's law. Look at the beasts of our farm; look at the wild animals in the woods!"

"Oh pity! I know not what I feel, but I want thee for myself alone, unshared by any other. Why imitate the animals, and do like others? Are we not sufficient to one another? Dost thou expect ever to be loved as by thy Gerard? Let us suspend, as far as we are concerned, prolific creation. Are not enough creatures born? Let us live for ourselves, for us two alone. Stephen, have pity; it is thyself I want, all to myself, thee alone! I know not what thou art, whether thou'rt a man like others, but to me thou'rt incomparable. Oh, why had she need to come between us? No, I am explaining myself ill; thy astonished eyes kill me! Listen, I suffer throughout my whole body, when I know thou'rt with her. Tormenting heat runs through all my blood. Your joined hands furrow softly within my bosom and lacerate my heart with your nails! Oh, my little Stephen, I die to think that she will kiss thee on the lips, that she will carry thee away far from here, and that I must give thee up for ever to this robber of my life.

"Stephen smiled, a little saddened withal, endeavouring his best to make him reasonable. "Big madman," said he "my feelings for thee will in no wise change. See, am I not always the same? We will meet as in the past. Thou shalt accompany me with her."

"But this reasoning had no effect on the poor shepherd.

"As the fatal day approached, Gerard pined away, lost his appetite, cared for nothing that he had attended to before, and neglected his flock. His ways became so alarming that his master and mistress sent him to the vicar. Perhaps someone had cast a spell on him! Shepherds all are somewhat sorcerers and themselves exposed to the evil practices of their fellows. The frank Gerard told the priest quite simply of his deep distress. But at the first word the holy man heard, he cried out: "Get thee gone, accursed man; thy presence is a plague. I know not what hinders me from handing thee over to the drossard of my Lord, the Duke of Brabant, and to have thee burnt in the Market-Place, as is done to others of thy kind. Thou must depart on the spot. Thy crime has cut thee off from the community of the faithful. None can absolve thee except the Pope of Rome. Throw thyself at his feet. As yet thou hast only sinned in thought. Were it otherwise I would call down on thy accursed flesh the flames of the purifying pile!"

"Gerard returned to his master's house, without shame, but more in despair than ever. He took good care not to relate in detail what had taken place between the minister of God and himself, but confined himself to declaring that he was going to undertake a long pilgrimage to expiate a deadly sin. That very night he would start when all were asleep, so as not to meet indiscreet or inquisitive persons. As a last favour he begged Stephen to accompany him a certain distance from their cottage. Wanna wished to detain her betrothed, but Stephen took pity on his friend, and in presence of a separation perhaps eternal, he remembered their long and unclouded love of days gone by.

"Brother, what is the fault so serious that causes thee to part?" inquired Stephen several times, as he walked along with his faithful companion. But the other was silent, simply giving him a long look and shaking his head.

"For a long time they walked on, sore at heart, without exchanging a word, but when they reached the crossroads where they were to embrace for the last time, Gerard turned round and showed Stephen a red light on the horizon, in the direction from which they had come.

"Then with a wild laugh, he said: "Look there, it is the old people's house that is in flames; and Wanna, thy Wanna, is burning with them! Now thou belong'st to me for ever!"

"And he embraced, with frantic energy the young man, who struggled to get free. "Gerard! Thou frightenest me! Help. The wolfman! He's throttling me!"

"Be mine. 'Twas I who gave thee life. I am more than thy mother, do'st understand? More therefore, than any woman, no matter who she be! Thou demandest the secret reason of my departure. Thou shalt know. Their priest has cursed me. I am decreed to eternal fire. Well, I hasten to plunge myself in advance into this fire, but not before imbibing the very sources of thy life, not before satiating myself with the sweets of thy lips, that succulent fruit which shall quench my thirst in the heart of the infernal furnace! Be mine! Mine! Mine!

"A sudden storm flung itself loose the while the wretched man broke out thus in cries of vengeance to heaven.

"Ah," rejoiced he, "fire of chastisement, be my fire of joy! Nature, burn me, consume me! Whether thou com'st, as they say, from God, or from the Devil, what matters it to me! Come, join us in the arms of death! Rise, beautiful storm of deliverance! I have naught else to lose; the fiery torrents shall be like to my flesh, fresh and limpid streams, compared with the love that devours me and has reduced me to despair!

"Ah, come!" And the accursed man pressed Stephen to his heart, stifling him, fastened his lips on his and withdrew them not again, until heaven's fire had enveloped them both."

At this point in the pathetic improvisation, Kehlmark's voice died away in a low murmur, like a gasp.

"Oh, my dear child," groaned he, falling at the feet of the young shepherd, "I love thee to distraction; as much as Gerard loved Stephen, so love I thee."

"And I, I love you also, dear master, and that with all my strength," replied Guidon, throwing his arms around his neck. "I am yours, yours alone, without a second thought. Is it only now that you know it? Do with me whate'er you will."

"I had but only to see thee," said Kehlmark, "to take compassion on thy beauty ignored and proudly chaste. And from that compassion sprang my love."

"And I, my dear master," stammered little Govaertz, "I had only to see you to know that you were sad and terrible, and my devotion was born of my anxiety."

"The pretended evil that thy father spake of thee, "resumed the Dykgrave," decided my sympathy, and thy sister's disdainful air, the malevolence of her look, illuminated thee henceforth in my eyes with a permanent light of transfiguration. . . I did not dare to declare myself before seeing thee again, and I feigned indifference so as to mislead thy family and thy over-rough comrades, whom that very evening I hindered, simply by approaching their turbulent band, from tormenting thee, my child, my life's chosen."

No lightning shaft struck them, but they heard a muffled cry, a sob, a rustling in the bushes behind them. Two indistinct silhouettes fled through the darkness.

"Somebody was listening to us!" said Kehlmark, who had stood up and was prying into the thick darkness.

"What does it matter? I am yours," murmured Guidon, drawing him towards him, and nestling shiveringly against his breast. "You are all for me, and I do not believe in the fire from heaven! Before thee, nobody ever said to me a single good word. I had known naught save reproaches and rough treatment. Thou art my master and my love. Do with me whatsoe'er thou wilt. . . Thy lips. . ."

V

A few days after this alarm in the gardens, Blandine presented herself to Kehlmark, engaged in writing, alone in his study.

Long had she hesitated before resolving on a step, which she considered indispensable, but the gravity of which she could not disguise from herself.

However, although she suffered a thousand deaths, her only thought was to put Kehlmark on his guard, forewarn him against the consequences of his too exclusive attachment to that wretched little vagabond. She refused to believe even her ears as to the extent of his passion; she persisted in seeing therein only an inconsiderate caprice, especially as she knew the Dykgrave's excitability, and the curious rage and violence which he applied to all his undertakings, even his least actions, for he was nothing if not impulsive.

When she entered, the pallor and discomposure of her countenance surprised the Count of Kehlmark.

As soon as he had invited her to sit down and was informed of the object of her visit she began resolutely, without oratorical preliminaries, but with a tight throat.

"I have thought it my duty, Count, to warn you that people outside begin to busy themselves over the continual presence of the son of Govaertz here at Escal-Vigor. Let us say nothing of his coming to the château, but I fear, Henry, that you really display too publicly an outrageous attachment to this little peasant before his equals outside."

"Blandine!" said Kehlmark, pushing away his papers, throwing aside his pen and standing up, confounded at the audacity of this introduction.

"Oh, pardon me, Monsieur Henry," she resumed, "I know well that your actions do not concern them. But all the same, people are so talkative! Always seeing this young peasant hanging at your heels sets their fancies and their evil tongues to work."

"That's a precious thing for me to trouble about!" cried the Count with a forced laugh. "What think you I care for that? Indeed, Blandine, you astonish me by thus concerning yourself with vulgar rumours. It is really showing too much condescension to the envious wretches."

"All the same, Monsieur Henry," she continued with a little less assurance, "I confess to you that I think the astonishment of the villagers well enough founded. Frankly, notwithstanding his qualities, this little

Guidon is not the companion for you. Admit it! You now see no one but him, or else you run about here and there with the Klaarvatsch vagabonds at the other end of the island. Of your old friends not one is now invited to Escal-Vigor. All that is not natural and leads to plenty of gossip. Others, besides coarse, ill-disposed people, have reason to be astonished at it."

"Blandine!" interrupted the Dykgrave in an icy and haughty tone, "since when have you taken it into your head to control my actions and interfere with the company I keep?"

"Oh, do not be angry, Monsieur Henry," she said, quite crushed by his harsh tone and forbidding look, "I know I am only your humble servant but I always love you," she continued weeping, "I am quite devoted to you. I would not go against your will in anything, but your reputation and illustrious name are dearer to me and more sacred than my own conscience. It is my great love alone that inspires my words. Ah Henry, if you only knew!"

Sobs prevented her from continuing.

"Blandine," said the Dykgrave, with more gentleness, pitying her grief, "what is the matter with you? Once more, I don't understand you. Explain yourself, do."

"Well, Count, not only do the people of the village laugh at your strange affection for this little shepherd, but some go so far as to assert that you divert him from his duties to his family. And what do they not invent besides! In short, everybody sees it in an evil light that you thus cherish a wretched little cowboy."

"And you, yourself, have not you kept cows? How proud you've become!" said the Dykgrave, cruelly.

"I am proud of belonging to you, Count, and then the Countess—" Blandine hesitated.

"My grandmother?" inquired the Count.

"Your sainted grandparent, my protectress, brought me up and taught me to love you," she went on with a touching inflection of the voice, which made Kehlmark's heart contract.

"Yes, I know that right enough, my poor Blandine. I also love thee and trust thee entirely. That is why I am surprised to see thee agree so well with the envious and malicious. . . I have nothing to reproach myself with, be sure of that. The same protection which my grandmother accorded thee I further bestow today on this young peasant. And is it thou who would'st make a crime of the good I wish to do to this despised and disinherited child? Ah Blandine, I no longer recognise thee in such a rôle. Guidon is an admirably gifted boy and of quite an exceptional nature. He interested me from the day I first saw him."

"That accursed night of the serenade!"

The Count pretended not to have heard these bitter words and went on:—

"It has pleased me to train him, to instruct him, to make him a son of my mind, to share all my knowledge with him. What is there blameworthy in that? I love him."

"You love him too much!"

"I love him as it pleases me to love him."

"Oh Henry! Twin brothers do not cling to one another as you seem to do to this obscure little shepherd. No, listen to me; do not be angry with what I am going to say; but I do not think you have ever loved a woman as much as this wretched boy. Wait, you shall know all. . . The other evening I slipped into the copse behind the bank on which you were both seated. I overheard the burning and terrible things which you uttered to him with such a voice—Ah! a voice that would have torn out my bowels! . . . I was still there when you gave him a long kiss on the mouth, and when after you had dragged yourself to his knees, he threw himself in an ecstasy on to your bosom."

"Ah," said Kehlmark in a rage, "you stooped so low, Blandine. Spying! All my congratulations!"

And fearing to give way to his anger, after crushing her with a condemnatory glance, he prepared to leave the apartment. But she flung herself at his knees and seized his hands:

"Forgive me, Henry; but I could not go on any longer. I wished to know. At first I refused to believe my eyes and ears. Have pity! Pity on yourself, Count. You have enemies. The minister Bomberg watches you and is eager to ruin you. Do not wait till an imprudence on your part gives him an opportunity. Cease compromising yourself. Others besides myself might have spied on you that evening. Abandon this unhappy child; send him back to his cow-dung and stalls. There is still time. Beware of a scandal. Get rid of this rascally fellow before people say aloud what doubtless many begin to think and to murmur low."

"Never!" cried Kehlmark, with an almost savage energy. "Never, do you hear? Once more, I have done no harm; on the contrary I desire only this child's good. Nothing, therefore, shall separate me from him."

"Very well, it is I who will go, then," said she, rising. "If this ill-fated little shepherd again sets foot in Escal-Vigor I leave you."

"As you will. I shall not detain you."

"Oh, Henry," she cried, "can it so be? You have then no longer the least kind feeling for me. He dismisses me, Oh God!"

"No, I do not dismiss you, but I permit no one to dictate terms to me. If those who profess to love me will not agree to live amicably together, but raise jealousies among themselves, I separate myself from her who has uttered threats and conspired enviously against another being who is dear to me. That is all. I have lived and will always live free as regards my sympathies and inclinations. For the rest," he continued, taking her by the hand, and looking at her with an ineffable expression of pride and defiance, "remember how I warned you before coming here into exile. I wished to separate from you. Have you forgotten your promise?—'I will be nothing but your faithful housekeeper and will not importune you in anything.'—I yielded to your entreaties, but not without foreseeing that you would repent of not having abandoned me to my destiny. What has happened justifies me. This experiment is sufficient, I think. Come, Blandine, without rancour, this time the moment has come to part for ever."

What was it that she read so poignant, so critical in the Dykgrave's look.

"No, no, I will not," she cried. "I repeat my former promise. Thou wilt see, Henry, I will keep my word. Oh, do not tear me away all at once from thy presence and thy heart!"

"So be it," Kehlmark consented, "let us try again, but thou must agree with Guidon Govaertz. He is the being whom I cherish most in this world, he is as necessary to me as the air I breathe; only he has reconciled me to life. And, above all, never an allusion before him to what has passed between us. Beware of showing the least animosity, of making the least reproach, to this child. If aught of ill happ'd to him, if I lost him, if he were taken from me in any way whatever, it would be suicide for me. Dost understand?"

She bent her head in sign of submission, decided to endure the worst tortures, but from *his* hands, beneath *his* eyes.

VI

In appearance, the conditions of life at Escal-Vigor, the relations between Kehlmark, Blandine, the young Govaertz and Landrillon underwent no alteration.

The valet, being ignorant of the explanation which Blandine had had with the Count, believed her to be entirely won over to his projects, and never ceased to present to her in an odious light the relations between the Dykgrave and his favourite. She was forced to listen to his hateful jests and to push dissimulation so far as to pretend to agree with the wretch. Further, Landrillon pressed her to surrender herself to him. In face of Blandine's refusal, he became impatient: "Come, be kind," said he, "and I promise not to disturb his idyll with young Govaertz; if not, I'll not be able to answer for anything further."

Blandine did her best to amuse him, to gain time. She even went so far as to promise him marriage on condition of his keeping silence. "I accept the terms," he said, "but you must pay cash down."

"Oh, nonsense, there's no hurry," objected Blandine, "let us stay here a bit longer to add to our little hoard."

This virtuous woman, if ever there was one, let herself pass for a jade in the eyes of the rascal, who admired her for it only the more, never before having met with such hypocrisy and dissimulation. This duplicity delighted him, but not without also frightening him a little. Would not the rollicking wench after all be somewhat too "fast" for him? To Blandine's misfortune, he became more and more carnally enamoured of her. He would have so much liked "to draw a trifle on account," he said. Blandine now defended herself but half-heartedly, she eluded the consummation of the sacrifice, but could no longer escape it for any length of time. Landrillon redoubled his familiarities.

In truth, never had Blandine loved Henry de Kehlmark so much. Her sufferings then may be imagined. On the one side, exposed to the enterprises of an execrable clown and obliged to flatter his hatred of the Dykgrave: and on the other, forced to witness the close intimacy and communion of Kehlmark and the young Govaertz.

Atrocious heart-rendings! At times, nature and instinct fought to resume their sway: she was on the point of denouncing Landrillon to his master; but the domestic if dismissed, would have avenged himself on Kehlmark by revealing what he called "his disgraceful conduct." At other times, Blandine, at the end of her strength, placed between the harrowing alternatives, either to give herself up to Landrillon or to ruin Kehlmark, had resolved to fly, to throw up the game; she even longed for death, thought of casting herself into the sea, but her love for the Count prevented her from putting such a project into execution. She could not abandon him to the snares of his enemies; she desired to protect him, to serve him as a shield and buckler against himself.

As she had to do terrible violence to herself not to show too much coldness to the young Govaertz, she avoided meeting with him, keeping out of his way and refrained as much as possible from coming to the table. She explained these absences by alleging headache.

"What can be the matter with Madame Blandine?" the little Guidon asked his friend. "I see such a strange look in her eyes."

"A slight indisposition; nothing at all; it will pass. Don't worry about it."

The poor woman often went about the house, like a lunatic, banging the doors and oversetting the furniture with great noise, through an impulse to break something or to cry aloud her intolerable pain; but, if she encountered Kehlmark he daunted and subdued her with a look.

One day, when Landrillon had particularly enervated her by threatening that he would no longer spare Kehlmark unless she gave herself up to him, she escaped once more from his odious importunities, and her head a little over-balanced, made a sudden irruption into the studio where the Count was sitting with his pupil. Her feelings were beyond her control. She could not resist casting a glance of disapproval at the peasant boy. The two friends were in the act of reading. None of the three said a word. But never was silence fuller of menace. She retired immediately, alarmed at the consequences of her intrusion.

"Blandine, you forget our agreement," said Kehlmark the first time he found himself alone with her.

"Forgive me, Henry, I can go on no longer. I have presumed too much on my strength. You love nobody but him. The rest of the world has ceased to exist for you. You scarcely accord me a look or a word."

"Well, yes," said he, resolutely, with a certain solemnity, and with the courage of the stoic holding his hand over the flames of the brazier. "Yes, I love him above everything. Outside of him I see for myself no salvation."

"Love another woman; yes, if thou art weary of me, take that Claudie, who longs for thee with all her boiling blood, but—"

"But I swear to thee that this child suffices for me!" "Oh, it is not possible!"

"I love him, I shall never love but him."

Kehlmark knew that he was dealing a terrible blow to his companion, but he himself was worn out; the weapon with which he struck he turned again into his own wound; he must have passed through such torments that he was in the situation of one who is damned, eager to share his punishment with others.

"Ah," he continued, "thou wishest to separate me from this child! So much the worse for thee! Thou shalt see at once how I detach myself from me. And to begin, this is my reply to thy appeals. Henceforth, Guidon shall leave me no more; he shall live in the chateau for good."

"Take care; I suffer to such an extent that I may do thee harm without intending it. There are moments when I feel myself going mad, when I can no longer answer for myself."

"How then, about me!" sneered the Dykgrave, "I am at the end of my patience. Thou hast wished it; thou hast forced me to come to these extremities. I spared thee; I confined myself to suffering alone; in order not to afflict thee I hid my sore, my secret. Unhappy Blandine, I dealt with thee gently convinced that thou also would'st refuse to understand me and would'st deny me. Thou hast wished to know; thou shalt know all. Be at ease, I will now conceal nothing from thee. Henceforth no further need to spy on me. Thy jealousy did not deceive thee: it is indeed love, the most absolute love, with which I love young Guidon. . . I adore him."

She uttered a cry of horror. The fond mistress and the Christian in her were equally shocked.

"Oh, Henry, for pity's sake; thou'rt not telling the truth; thou could'st not so degrade thyself.

"Degrade myself! On the contrary, I am proud of it!"

There were scenes more and more violent between them. Blandine yielded, submitted, divided between horror and infinite compassion, which, when united, form one of the most corrosive forms of love.

Guidon now slept at the château. Blandine avoided him, but she showed herself at times to Kehlmark, and such was the expression of her face that at sight of her the Count broke out into reproaches.

"Take care, Blandine," he said to her on another occasion, "you are playing a dangerous game. Without loving you in the way of love, I have devoted to you a sort of worship based on profound gratitude. I revered you as I have never revered any woman save my grandmother.

"But in the end I shall execrate you. By placing yourself always as an obstacle in the path of my desires, you will become as odious to me as an executioner, who should take it into his head to deprive me of food and sleep. Ah, you are doing a fine, charitable work, you holy, virtuous, angelic woman!

"With thy airs and mute reproaches, thy face of Our Lady of Seven Sorrows, if I die mad thou mayest boast of being the chief extinguisher of my reason.

"For more than a year hast thou spied on me, thwarted me, harassed me, and burnt my very heart over a slow fire, under pretence of loving me."

—"Why did you seduce me?" she asked him.

—"Seduce thee! Thou wert no virgin!" he had the wickedness to fling back in reply.

"Fi, Monsieur! in speaking to me thus you are more brutal than the poor wretch who outraged me. You are more guilty than he, because you possessed me without joy and without love.

"Oh, why?"

"I WISHED TO CHANGE MYSELF, to conquer myself, to overcome my inveterate repugnances, he replied. Thou art the only woman indeed whom I have possessed; the only one who went near to stirring my blood."

VII

After these scenes Kehlmark often reproached himself. "Never will anybody love me whole-heartedly like this woman," he said arguing with himself. And he recalled their first intimacy in the grandmother's house. He had always been her oracle, her god. She was his advocate with the Dowager, palliated his follies, and obtained for him money which he needed. Where would he meet with such devotion and faithfulness again? Did she not now even go the length of tolerating his passion for young Govaertz?

Then, at the height of his good dispositions, a complete reaction would take place. For a word, a look, an intonation of voice, for anything he thought he noticed of severity, or disapproval in her face, he began again to suspect and even to detest her, seeing only in her devotion a diseased, inquisitorial curiosity, a refinement of vengeance and contempt. She exercised her wits, he imagined, to confound and overwhelm him by her self-abnegation. This angel was to him but a skilful torturer.

And, on the first occasion, the unhappy man broke out into invectives against her, of an increasingly atrocious character.

At this period, Blandine's beauty reflected the superhuman exaltation of her sentiments; her beauty had something in it even of the majesty of death. But a repose and peace even more absolute than that of the tomb was about to reign in her heart.

Harassed by Landrillon, she had ended by giving herself up to him. She had offered her poor body as a holocaust to save the soul of him whom she regarded as sacreligious and criminal. As a Christian woman she doubtless prayed for him to snatch his soul from perdition, and all her heart rose towards the ungrateful man at the very moment when she immolated herself in the arms of the odious blackmailer.

The sacrifice was renewed at each fresh exigency of the rascal. Blandine breathed again. Landrillon would not attempt anything against the Count's reputation. She hoped also for a miracle. Kehlmark would recover from his error. Heaven would hear the saint's prayer.

Weeks went by. "Look here! We have been taking our fill of pleasure together for some time now, my girl, but it's not simply a question of frivolity," said Landrillon one day. "We must think of serious matters; and to begin with, we are going to get married."

"Bah! Is that really necessary," said the woman, with a forced laugh.

"What a question! Whether it is necessary? Thou'rt my mistress; and thou'dst refuse to be my wife!"

"What's the good, seeing thou hast had me—"

"What's the good'? Why, I want to become thy husband. For the rest, what dost thou hope for still in staying here?"

"Nothing!"

"Very well, then let's be off. Enough of pickings and scrapings! It's time to combine our little savings by going before the notary, and then, before the vicar. After that, good evening, Monsieur le Comte de Kehlmark."

"Never!" said she, with savage energy, thinking of the two others, and with a fixed stare, far away from her interlocutor.

"Why, what's the matter with'ee? And our agreement, what dost with that? I want thee for my lawful splice. Thou hast some ha'pence. I must have'em. Or dost thou prefer that I reveal the chaste mysteries of Escal-Vigor to Balthus Bomberg and Claudie Govaertz?"

"Thou'lt not do that, Landrillon!" "Ah, we'll see if I won't!"

"I make a proposal," she said. "I'll give thee the money; I will give thee all I have; but let me live here, and you look for another wife."

"Can it be that thou lov'st him still, then, thy buggaboo?" exclaimed the rascal. "So much the worse. Thou'st got to make up thy mind to leave him and become Madame Landrillon. No nonsense! Thou hast two months to think it over, and then chuck it all!"

Abandon Escal-Vigor! Never see Kehlmark again!

As fate willed it, at the height of her anguish, the unhappy woman encountered Henry de Kehlmark, who, provoked by her scared, dolorous look, took her again to task.

"That's a face like a funeral once more! Of course, it's settled. I am the most monstrous of men! But then, Blandine, art not thou thyself a monster to attach thyself to such a being as I?"

"And who knows," jeered the unhappy man, with the sardonic sneer of a wretch exposed to torture, "if it is not my exceptional nature, my alleged anomaly, which flatters thy imaginings? Who will prove to me that in thy devotion there is not an element of sexual perversion, as the sciolists say; something of that pleasure in suffering, which they call by the pretty name of Masochism? In that case thy beautiful self-sacrifice would only stand for madness and disease for some, and crime and disgrace in the eyes of others. Oh, virtue! Oh, sanity! Where are you?"

Never before had he gone at her with such bitter onslaught.

"Alas!" she mused, "to think that it is I who cause him so much misery. I who no longer know what to give up for him; I who, for the sake of his peace, have agreed to live such a life, O Lord!"

"Henry, my dear Henry," she implored him, be silent, O my God! be silent. Only say what thou wishest me to do? I am nothing but thy servant, thy slave. What hast thou still to reproach me with?"

"Thy contempt, thy grimaces, thy saintly airs! Go, leave me; abandon this plague-stricken man. I want no more of thy insulting compassion. Ah, thou art my remorse, my living reproach. Whatever thou dost thou art a mirror in which I see myself constantly fastened to the pillory, under the red-hot iron of the executioner."

And, seizing her by the wrists at the risk of bruising them, he shouted in her face: "O normal, irreproachable woman, I hate thee, dost hear, I hate thee!

"Go, I have had enough. Any extremity rather than this hell. Betray me, Madame Judas. Rouse our virtuous neighbours and the whole island. Run to the minister. Tell them what I am. Ah! It's all the same to me.

"This perpetual lying, this constant deception stifles me and weighs upon my spirits. Anything rather than this torture. If thou dost not speak, I'll speak myself; I will tell them all. Ah! I seem infamous to thee; but then, Blandine, thou art more infamous than I, for having lived at the expense of him whom thou despisest, for allowing thyself to he fed and kept by such a reprobate, for having so long tolerated his vices, because he paid thee liberally!"

"Henry, my beloved! Dost thou really believe that? Oh! How thou would'st blame thyself, how horrified thou would'st be if thou knew'st the truth."

Ah, yes, how unjust he was. The injustice of which he believed himself the victim, made him frenzied, blind, and cruel as fate.

He confounded with the crowd,—the malevolent, conforming mass,—this admirable woman, this magnanimous mistress, at times awkward or lacking in strength, presuming too much on her powers, however heroic, and driven to extremity she also, but drawing from her love fresh means of exalting more and more this god, who banished her from his heaven.

"Yes, I do believe it, truly!" persisted the deluded man; "Thou sparest me, thou'rt careful of me, because thou lead'st here a lady's life, and because thou think'st thyself indispensable to such a prodigal, this spendthrift, who never learned to count. Thou fanciest I cannot do without thee. Thou'rt mistaken. Go away. Leave me to ruin myself in health, goods, and honour. Thou'rt rich enough. Rid me of thy presence! . . . I'll give thee money even. But for the love of heaven, get gone as quickly as possible. Things that can never be undone have passed between us. Henceforth we must have a mutual horror of one another."

"Oh! my Henry!" sobbed out the poor woman.

She was going to speak, but her words would have confounded and humiliated him, and she retired so as not to be tempted to tell him the truth.

VIII

L eft alone, the idea came to Kehlmark for the first time to look over his account books and inform himself at first hand of the state of his affairs. He had given his procuration to Blandine. It was she who managed his fortune. He knew the cabinet in which she locked up the documents relative to the accounts. The key was not in the drawer; but, without hesitation, he broke the lock and set to work rummaging among the papers and examining columns of figures and notary's deeds. Before he reached the end of his investigations he saw the truth: he was as good as ruined. Escal-Vigor was almost the only one of his estates not hypothecated. But whence came the money then by which his luxury, liberalities, and princely mode of life were kept up?

What generous banker advanced him such considerable sums without security and without the least chance of being ever repaid?

All at once he understood.

It was Blandine! Blandine! whom he had just insulted so grossly. The rôles were reversed. He was the kept man, the guest! Instead of calming him, this discovery in his then state of mind only exasperated him.

At the height of passion to which he had risen nothing could balance the injustice of which he had to complain.

He again attacked the young woman:

"Better and better," he said; "I know all. Thou wouldst buy me; support me; no longer do I possess an available penny. Escal-Vigor ought by rights to belong to thee; it will hardly represent the value of the sums thou hast given me. But, my dear, you have made a wrong calculation in flattering yourself thus to bind me to you and make me your loyal vassal. No, no, I am not for sale. I will depart from this place. I will leave you the château. I want nothing from you."

"Then," he continued, with atrocious banter, as though he were torturing himself, "after what I have confessed to thee thou would'st have made a sorry purchase in my person. Ah! Ah! Ah!

"Our mutual situation is even more extraordinary than I thought. It takes a lot to turn *thy* stomach. But, little fool, with the money left thee by my grandmother thou'dst have been able to obtain a real male, a solid woman-fancier. Ah, I have it! Thou'dst have no need to look a great way off. This Landrillon—"

Unhappy Kehlmark.

In his desire of revolt and revenge he had just caused Blandine the worst of wounds. Ah, the wretched man! He did not yet suspect the greatest of the sacrifices she had made for him. The loss of her fortune was nothing in comparison with this other holocaust. What demon had just brought to Kehlmark's comminatory lips the last name he should have pronounced?

Kehlmark was never to know how abominable he had shown himself at that moment, but scarcely had the name of Landrillon left his mouth than a pang passed through him; the pale face and beseeching eyes of Blandine revealed to him a part of the blow which he had just dealt her.

He caught the swooning woman in his arms.

"It was not I who spoke just now, my darling. Forgive me, it is a past of ineffable pain and secret shame; it is my exasperated senses which are avenging themselves."

And to win her pardon, he made a general confession to her, or rather, drew her a complete picture of his inner life.

Whilst recalling his dark hours he became once more, as erstwhile, cruel and aggressive, but then would again caress her; and his sardonic excitement bordered at times on madness.

"Ah, Blandine! Blandine! how much I have suffered and still suffer no one will ever know, who has not passed through the same terrors.

"Poor darling, that thought I was angry with thee and that I took pleasure in hurting thee. But see, be reasonable. Thou hast before thee a person tied at the stake, burning over a slow fire, and it's thou who would'st reproach him with the atrocious spectacle his sufferings inflict on sensitive souls? Ah, a spectacle that he shows thee indeed against his will!

"And it is this martyred victim, this patient sufferer, whose whole being is a perpetual torture, an agonising irritation, it's this man burnt alive whom thou'dst accuse of being thy executioner.

"Henceforth, O sister mine, spare him thy shocked looks, thy virtuous disapprobation.

"Ah, I've had enough of it. Seeing I have hurt thee unwittingly, the best of women, for what reason, I wonder, should I spare the feelings of the crowd. Far from humbling myself, I'll hold up my head.

Would'st thou judge me, condemn me like the rest? Be it so! But I contest even thy right to absolve me. I am neither diseased nor guilty. I feel my heart bigger and spirit broader than their most boasted apostles. Therefore do not play the pharisee towards me, O Blandine! my irreproachable one.

"Above all, a truce to those insulting and withering words when speaking of my loves—my only possible loves.

"Those words, O angel mine, that made thee in a moment lose all the benefits of thy whole past life of kindness and good sense. Enough of a devotion that burns as with a hot iron! Enough of cauteries!"

"Henry," the poor woman groaned," let us not go back into the past. Tear out my heart, but speak never again to me like that. It is all done with. Far from blaming thee, I now more than excuse thee, I approve. Is it that thou wishest of me? Why, I will damn myself with thee, I'll renounce my baptism, the sacred gospel, Jesus, all!"

He scarcely heeded her; he burst forth, opening all the sluices of his heart.

She, transfigured, had made him sit down in an armchair; made him a necklace of her arms, and cheek by cheek they mingled their tears. But she, being aware that Kehlmark's despair had precedence, was greater even than her own, took up none but a maternal attitude.

"Tell me, Blandine," said he, "to whom have I ever done harm? To thee? But without meaning it; I was not at all the man thou had'st dreamed of, or at least, the sort thou would'st have wished. I cannot help it. The first to suffer was I myself through thy suffering. Thou weep'st in listening to me; thou art right, Blandine, if thou shed'st these tears at the thought of my calvary, of my long Passion. Thy pity does me honour and does me good. But, if it be from shame for me that thou weep'st, my darling, if thou condemn'st and renouncest me, if thou sharest the prejudice of this western and Protestant world—Oh, then, abandon me, stop thy tears; I have naught to do with sympathy of which thou'rt ashamed.

"Yes, from today onwards I'll no longer fear the opinions of men, have no more cowardly modesty, Blandine.

"A time will come when I'll proclaim my *raison d'être* in face of all the world. . .

"It is high time. My hell has lasted long enough. It commenced at puberty. Sent to college, my boyish friendships took on all the tenderness, vivacity, and melancholy of true love. At the baths, the quivering nudity of my comrades induced in me a troublous but delicious ecstasy. In drawing from the antique I revelled in the noble male models; a born Pagan, I could think of no good quality without clothing it in the harmonious forms of an athlete, of a youthful hero or a young god; and voluptuously, I attuned the dreams and aspirations of my soul to the hymning of the glory of athletic limbs. At the same time, cocks and pheasants I thought more beautiful than their hens, lions and tigers more imposing than lionesses and tigresses. But I kept silence and concealed my predilections. I even tried to impose on my eyes and my other senses; I did violence to my heart and my flesh to convince them of their error and the aberration of their sympathies. Thus, at the boarding-school, I loved to desperation William Percy, a young English lord (the same who almost drowned me) without ever daring to show him, otherwise than by a brotherly affection, the ardour with which I was consumed for him. On leaving Bodemberg Schloss, when I met thee, Blandine, I hoped through my love for thee, to enter again into the common order. But, unfortunately for us both, this encounter was only an accident in my sexual life. In spite of loyal and heroic efforts, and a determined concentration of will, to fix my affections on the best and most desirable of women, the promptings of my flesh soon turned away from thee and I no longer loved thee Blandine save with my whole soul! At this period some remains of Christian, or rather Biblical scruples, caused me to feel disgusted with myself. I felt horror at my own being and verily believed that I was curséd, possessed, and destined to the fires of Sodom!

"Then the injustice, the iniquity of my destiny, reconciled me tacitly to myself. I arrived at the pitch of accepting in my innermost heart nothing except the testimony of my own conscience. Strong in my absolute integrity, I revolted against the amorous disposition that prevails in the great majority. Reading further enlightened me as to the meaning and legitimacy of my inclinations. Artists, philosophers, heroes, kings, popes, even gods, justified and exalted by their example the cult of male beauty. In my reaction from doubt and remorse, I read again, to confirm my sexual faith and religion, the ardent sonnets of Shakespeare to William Herbert, Earl of Pembroke, and those no less idolatrous, of Michael Angelo to Tommoso di Cavalieri; I fortified myself by perusing passages from Montaigne, Tennyson, Wagner, Walt Whitman and Carpenter; I recalled to my mind the young people of the Banquet of Plato, the lovers of the Sacred Band of Thebes, Achilles and Patroclus, Damon and Pythias, Hadrian and Antinous, Chariton and Melanippe, Diocles, Cleomachus,—I shared in all these generous, virile passions of antiquity and of the Renascence, that they boast to us about in such a ridiculously pedantical way at college, while glozing over the superb eroticism, inspirer of purest art, doughtiest deeds, and loftiest patriotism. "My external life, however, continued to be one perpetual constraint and dissimulation. I attained, through dint of unrighteous discipline, to a mastery of falsehood. But my upright and honourable nature never ceased to revolt against this imposture. Imagine, my dear friend, the awful antagonism between my open and expansive character and such a mask, belying and Vilifying my impulses and affinities! Ah, I may confess to thee now, that more than once, my carnal indifference to women threatened to turn into a veritable hate. And thou, Blandine mine, almost exasperated me against thy entire sex, thou, the best of women. The day, when thou thought'st to separate me from Guidon Govaertz, I felt my almost filial affection for thee changing into complete execration. Under these conditions, thou wilt understand that,—outraged often in my sentiments and isolated, practically anathematised,—I came nigh to losing my reason.

"More than once I trembled on the brink of complete aberration. Since I am taxed with monstrosity, I said to myself, since I am fallen and socially an outcast, I may as well enjoy the benefit of my ignominy.

"The sadistic enormities of a Gilles de Rais tempted my waking dreams.

"Dost thou remember the child thou did'st snatch one day from my arms? Mad with rage, I struck at thee with a knife, and yet never did'st thou guess what lay at the back of my mind! Another day, when we were still living in town, I accosted a young urchin of the harbour, a ragged boy, like the little ragamuffins of the Klaarvatsch beach. Urged by an abominable perversion I was going to carry him aside, behind a heap of bales.

"I lifted the brat into my arms; the little boy smiled broadly, in nowise afraid, although, at that moment, I must have had the congested face of an apoplectic strangled by asphyxia. The gentleman wished to play no doubt and would afterwards give him a coin. The child was as chubby as a peach, as brown as his ragged corduroys, and his chestnut eyes sparkled with a roguish twinkle. Whilst I hurried on, with dry throat, he began playfully to pull my beard. Then the sulphurous, bituminous veil was torn from my eyes. I remembered my childhood, my grandmother, thou, Blandine, my angel! No, no! I put the youngster down and fled. Since then I have repelled those sinister suggestions engendered by the Catholic faith. No, do not deflower innocence, or at least spare weakness, I said to myself. Breathe only the perfume which exhales towards thee. Take no advantage of the self-ignorant child, or of the future male!

"Soon after this my grandmother died. I determined to set to work to search for the being whom I could love according to my nature; that is why I exiled myself to, this island; I had the presentiment of meeting here my elect. Guidon had only to show himself for my heart to leap at once towards him. I recognised in him aptitudes for the arts that I love, elevated ideas and sentiments on life, of a kind different from those of the downtrodden crowd. Besides, how could I remain indifferent to the mute and delicate entreaty of his eyes? He had divined me as well as I had forefelt him. He was the first and the only one to satisfy the first need of my being. If our flesh has done aught ill, the most complete moral fervour was our accomplice. Our feelings coincided with our desires.

"But no, Nature disavows nothing, denies nothing which renders us happy. It is the Biblical religions which will have it that the earth has produced us for abstinence and pain. Imposture! He would be an execrable Creator who would take pleasure in the torture of his creatures. At this rate, the worst of sadisms would be that of a pretended God of love. Our punishment would form his pleasure!

"Now, can'st thou understand my life and wilt comprehend why I speak so proudly to thee, notwithstanding the splendour of thy soul, Blandine.

"Thou hast known friends of mine, of my own class, excellent people, a chosen few, capable of every indulgence and of all understanding, thinkers, minds of the first rank, whom no speculation, even the most daring, seemed likely to alarm. Thou wilt recollect how they sought me. Well, remember my sudden fits of sadness in their otherwise gay company, my prolonged absences from home, my apparent bouts of sulkiness. What was the cause? In the midst of lively conversation, at the height of our confidences and frank disclosures, it occurred to me what welcome would these self-same friends give me if they could read my soul, if they had any suspicion of my peculiarity. And, at the bare idea, I revolted inwardly against that opprobrium with which they would not have failed to visit me, "advanced" and audacious as they pretended to be. The most generous, while refraining from blame, would have shunned me like a leper. How often in less cultivated circles, when I heard people speak with withering contempt and with horrible words and gestures, of lovers of my sort, was I not on the point of bursting out and proclaiming my identity with the alleged transgressors and spitting in the face of these merciless honest people!

"And my sufferings also, when the conversation turned on gallantry and good fortunes! Forced to laugh and to join in the competition of licentious stories and to relate in my turn, a broad jest or a feat of libertinism, I felt my heart rise and I reproached myself for my base compliance.

"The "Fire Shepherd," whose legend lately thou heard'st me relate, refused to go on pilgrimage to Rome to throw himself at the feet of the Pope and implore his pardon. That sinner repudiated any arbiter between his conscience and the crowd. I was humbler. One day I wrote to an illustrious revolutionary, one of those torch-bearers, who pass for being in advance of their age and dream of a world of brotherhood, happiness and love. I consulted him on my state as though it concerned one of my friends. The man from whom I expected consolation, a reassuring word, a sign of tolerance, wrote me a letter of anathema and ban. He cried *raca* on the deserter of the ordinary moral love-code, showing himself as merciless to exceptional beings as the Pope of the legend was to the knight Tannhäuser. Ah! this pope of the new revolution vowed me for life to Venusberg, or rather to Uranienberg!

"This major excommunication, which should have made me despair, restored me to the sentiment of my personal dignity and my duties towards my own nature. I derived the strength to live conformably to my conscience and my needs, from the very injustice which was done me by humanity, but in my isolation I went through alternate crises of discouragement and revolt; and thou'lt understand now, dear one, my eccentric humours, my prodigalities and excesses, my break-neck exploits. Yes, I sought always for forgetfulness and more than once for death!"

"Thou hast suffered more than I," said Blandine, as he stopped, consoled, with a sort of serenity, his face almost blooming, lighted up with frankness, "but, thou shalt at least suffer no more by my fault. I am converted to thy religion of love; I strip off my last prejudices. I not only excuse, but I admire and exalt thee and I agree to whatever thou wilt. Be at thy ease, Henry, thou'lt never hear another complaint, much less a reproach. Guidon, whom thou lov'st with body and soul, shall be my friend; I will be his sister. We will leave this country if thou wilt, Henry; we will go and live elsewhere, we three, modestly, but henceforth, in peace and reconciliation."

GEORGES EEKHOUD

Amazed at so much self-sacrifice, the Dykgrave cried:

"Oh, to be unable to love thee, save as a mother, yet as a mother tenderer than the best, my saintly Blandine, but only a mother!" She stopped his words with this cry:—

"Ah, that is why something prevented me long ago from going to seek the other in his prison!"

There was triumph and rejoicing in the despair of Blandine. It was the sublime madness of sacrifice. The woman rose to the angel!

She was to rise still higher and to cast aside all carnal jealousy.

Adding deeds to words, she bade Kehlmark call Guidon, and when the young man appeared, she took his hands, placed them herself in those of the master and then let fall a kiss, chaste but as comforting as the salute of death, upon the blushing forehead of the disciple.

PART THE THIRD
THE FAIR OF ST. OLFGAR

I

As a result of this culminating explanation, the Dykgrave, to whom Blandine had revealed a part of Landrillon's manœuvres, namely, those of which she had not been directly the victim, dismissed the domestic.

The Count preferred to face the worst consequences of this step rather than continue to breathe the same air with the rascal, and Blandine, entirely won over to her master's views, now feared no longer the scandal that the fellow had constantly threatened.

Landrillon was stupefied at this unexpected execution. He believed he was about to attain his ends and that he held them both, Blandine and the Count, at his mere mercy. How dared they send him away? Truly he could not get over it.

But, although taken aback for the moment, when Kehlmark, having had him summoned, bluntly gave him his dismissal, his effrontery soon resumed its way:—

"Bless me, Count!" he exclaimed banteringly, "you think our relations will stop there! No, indeed! You will not so soon have done with me. A man knows plenty of things, who has not had his eyes and ears in his pocket."

"Low wretch!" exclaimed Kehlmark, staring steadily and imperiously at the rascal, who had thought to intimidate him, and making him to lower his eyes. "Get out! I don't care a jot for your plots. Know, however, that for the least defamation aimed at us, at myself or at the beings dear to me, I will make you responsible, and have you dragged up before the law-courts."

Then, as the varlet contracted his lips to vomit forth some unclean word, Kehlmark, with a sudden movement, thrust him outside head foremost, choking the insult down his throat.

Having packed his belongings, Landrillon, white with rage and breathing out vengeance, rejoined Blandine, flattering himself with the idea that he would be able to get back his own out of her and terrorise her for both.

"It's getting serious. They declare war against me now! Look out for yourself!" he came and said to her.

"You can do just as you please," replied Blandine, henceforth as calm and self-possessed as Kehlmark. "We shall be surprised at nothing from you!"

"We! We have then made it up with the. . . bugger. Let us be polite! Not weak stomached, the little 'un! We'll share him with his youngster, or, what shall we say to be always polite? An establishment of three! All my compliments!"

These insinuations failed to cause her the slightest emotion. She contented herself by regarding him with an air of contempt.

This impassibility completed the stupefaction of the groom.

The hussy was escaping him! Would he never have any more power over her? To make himself sure, he went on:

"But its no question of all that. Enough joking! Thou hast put thy name to a compact with me. I'm pitched out. Thou'st got to come with me!"

"Never!"

"How dost thee say that f Thou belong'st to me. Hast thou told thy miserable looking lord that thou had'st the shoving of a little pleasure with me? Or would'st like me to inform him?"

"He knows all," she said.

She lied purposely, so as to be able to parry any attack on Landrillon's part. If he spoke, the Count would not believe him. The noble creature desired Kehlmark always to remain ignorant to what a degree she had sacrificed herself for the sake of his tranquility; she wished to avoid humiliating him, or rather causing him everlasting remorse, by such a proof of how much she had loved him.

"What! and in spite of that he takes thee back again!" cried Landrillon. "Peuh! you are really worthy the one of the other. So thou still lov'st this broken-down swell?"

"Thou hast hit it exactly; and, if possible, more than ever."

"Thou belong'st to me. I want thee, and on the spot, were it only for the last time."

"No! Never again; I am free of you, and laugh henceforth at all your enterprises." Landrillon was so taken aback at this change of face and so daunted by the desperately resolute air of the owners of Escal-Vigor that once outside he dared not follow up his conspiracy and divulge what he had seen, or at least, speak of what he suspected.

In the village, he asserted that he had left Escal-Vigor of his own accord in order to establish himself, and, as his version was not contradicted from the château, this unexpected event did not occasion any great amount of gossip.

Not daring yet to break openly with his former master, he attempted to undermine his popularity. Accordingly, he paid assiduous court to Claudie, whom his free-handed joviality had always amused, and he flattered the vanity of the farmer of Les Pélérins. Rejected by Blandine, he pitched his choice on the rich heiress of the farm, but this new caprice he meant to employ in the service of the inextinguishable hatred which he bore henceforth to the Dykgrave's mistress,—one of those hates which represent the aberration of love. For he began madly to desire the woman, who had escaped and outwitted him.

Landrillon put in appearance also at the services and sermons of Dom Balthus. He insinuated himself into the good graces of the pastor's wife and of the two old maids, the sisters of the Les Pélérin's farmer.

The former valet did not dare yet to act openly, but he would yet let loose a terrible storm on Kehlmark, his concubine, and their favourite. Their pride, their audacity, astonished him; indeed had they "cheek and brass!" How could they reconcile such morals with dignity! Nothing more was wanting but that they should seek to derive glory from their disgrace!

The scamp was a better prophet than he knew. He thought he had the right to hold his old master in deep contempt. The thousand acts of blackguardism, to which he, a thoroughgoing rascally trooper, an absolute prostitute, had abandoned himself during his time served in a military prison, seemed to him mere trifles and of no consequence whatsoever. In all times vice has condemned true love, and the Kehlmarks have been the rehabilitation of the Landrillons. The crowd will always prefer Barabbas to Jesus.

As a beginning, Landrillon was going to apply himself to detaching Michael Govaertz from the lord of Escal-Vigor; to cool the fine enthusiasm of the father and daughter, to warm the rancour of the virago against Blandine, and then to incriminate vaguely the relations between Guidon and Kehlmark.

"In your place," he ventured to say one day to Michael and Claudie, "I would not leave the young Guidon at the château. The irregular household of the Count and this minx is a bad example for a young man."

He saw by their astonished smile that he was taking a wrong road and so did not press the point.

Landrillon would not have been able to furnish the proof of the scandalous imputations that he was burning to formulate against the master of Escal-Vigor. To think that for an instant the rascal had flattered himself to be able to produce Blandine against him?

Warned beforehand, the Count would hold himself on his guard, would have care not to take any compromising step, to fall into any traps, and would save appearances to perfection.

The presence of Guidon at the château was justified from every point of view. Far from parting with him, the Count had just taken him into his service as secretary.

For a moment, Thibaut thought of suborning witnesses, of corrupting the Klaarvatsch workmen, the five Hercules, whom the Count employed for the rough jobs in the château and who posed as models in his studio. But these rough simple fellows were devoted to their patron, and would have badly handled the enemy at the first word broached of his nefarious plan. It was necessary to use stratagem, to gain them in some other way, cautiously, without hurrying matters.

He confined himself, for the time, to canvassing those of Klaarvatsch, who did not work continuously at the château, the sculpturesque sailors, the supernumeraries of the athletic games and ornamental tourneys, the personages of the "masks" and living pictures arranged by the Dykgrave. Landrillon accordingly, instilled into them a feeling against the five privileged ones and especially against the little favourite, who took the principal parts in these masquerades, as they were called by the valet, who had himself been rigorously excluded from these aesthetic interludes on account of his vulgarity. The men ended by agreeing with Landrillon that the ascendency of that little, beardless brat, Guidon Govaertz, over the Dykgrave was far too great. Ill-disposed towards the page, it would not be long, calculated this Machiavel of the dunghill, before they regarded the master himself with a less favourable eye.

On the other hand, the quondam domestic, who had opened a sort of hostelry between the park of Escal-Vigor and the village of Zoudbertinge, drew the unfavourable notice of the notables upon the excessive interest manifested by Henry in the ragamuffins of Klaarvatsch, the refuse of the Isle of Smaragdis.

Landrillon now often saw Balthus Bomberg. But he confined himself to entertaining the latter with the equivocal relationship of Blandine and the Count, without giving him a glimpse of a still more shocking and enormous moral irregularity.

The minister, who had cudgelled his brains to find a means of overthrowing and ruining the Dykgrave, had never contemplated, even in imagination, a weapon so maleficent as that which Landrillon counted one day upon using. Ah, the terrible explosion! If that mine one day burst the worst scoundrels would be obliged to abandon the unworthy favourite! Not a decent man on the island would again hold out his hand to the reprobate!

"What are we to do, my dear Monsieur Landrillon," the vicar, meanwhile, asked of his new ally, "to exorcise and turn again these fanatics, so as to wean them from this sorcerer, this corruptor?"

"Yes, yes! Corruptor is not too harsh!" broke in Landrillon, with an inward laugh, which would have given much cause for suspicion to any other than this pastor, who, though a rigid moralist, was of limited ideas.

"Mind you," he protested, "I have no spite against this wicked nobleman; I am solely moved by zeal for my religion, proper morals, and the triumph of goodness."

"In order to succeed, my Reverend Sir," Landrillon resumed a cunning look, "we must discover in the Count of Kehlmark a transgression which would offend a terrible, and in some sort ineradicable, prejudice in our social and Christian order; you understand what I mean, an abomination which would cry not only for vengeance to heaven but even to the less hardened sinners."

"Yes, but who will furnish us the proof of a crime of this nature?" sighed Bomberg. "Patience, my Reverend Sir, patience!" snuffled artfully the wicked domestic.

Bomberg kept his ecclesiastical superiors informed as to the more favourable turn which their affairs were taking.

Constantly besieged by Landrillon, Claudie began to get impatient at the delays and procrastination of the Count of Kehlmark. What contributed the more to irritate her was that the rejected suitors round about did not scruple to laugh at her, and even caricature her in tavern songs. Landrillon made her believe that Blandine still retained her hold on the Dykgrave. Consequently, the gawky booby still more detested the housekeeper, the affected minx! Equally reserved with her as with Bomberg, Landrillon took care not to set the hot-blooded peasant girl yet upon the right track. "Ah, we shall see some rare fun the day that Claudie gets to know the truth. There'll be some fine milk spilt," mused the crafty sneak, rubbing his hand and laughing to himself!

He rejoiced in advance, tasted and gloated over his vengeance, took voluptuous pleasure in sharpening the decisive weapon, unwilling to strike except with sure blow, and in perfect safety for himself.

Claudie for her part, however, did not abandon her great project. She would win Kehlmark from her white-faced rival.

Seeing her still so smitten with the Dykgrave, Landrillon, whose watchful hate served him like a gift of divination, began by revealing to her the Count's financial difficulties; then he predicted the downfall of the great lord and even his early departure. Contrary to the valet's expectation, Claudie, although surprised, showed herself none the less inclined for the ruined gentleman. She almost rejoiced at this disaster, for she flattered herself to capture the Count, if not by love at least by money. From that moment she cherished a little project, which, in her judgment, must infallibly succeed, and of which she did not breathe a word to anybody.

If Kehlmark was ruined or nearly so, Claudie considered herself rich enough for both. Then, there still remained the title of Countess and the prestige attached to Escal-Vigor. The Govaertzes felt themselves equal to regilding the blazon of the Kehlmarks. Meanwhile they entered in appearance into the movement of disapproval started and encouraged by Landrillon against the Dykgrave, and even seemed ostensibly to countenance the varlet's proceedings.

In the parish, the wags did not scruple to say that out of spite at not being able to lay hold on the Count's coronet she had fastened on to the servant's livery.

Claudie's private plan was completely to isolate the Dykgrave, to set all Smaragdis against him, and then, when he should be reduced to impotence, she would appear to him like a providence. She would even foment a quarrel between Kehlmark and the Burgomaster and take back from him the young Guidon.

Already Kehlmark had handed in his resignation as Dykgrave and abandoned also his presidentships of associations and of social clubs, ceasing to interest himself in the community's doings. No further largesses; no more fêtes. Nothing more was needed to make him lose two-thirds of his popularity.

Claudie had become reconciled to the two sisters of her father without the latter's knowledge. Authorised and spurred on by their niece, they forced their brother to buckle under. "Thou must break with the master of Escal-Vigor, or thou'lt cause us to disinherit thy dear Claudie!"

Govaertz would perhaps have put his back up, but he had no right to compromise the future of his children. Claudie came to the rescue, declaring she no longer wished to become Countess. Moreover, she attacked her father on his vain side. Since the Count had returned to the country Michael Govaertz had counted for nothing. He was only Burgomaster in name.

Govaertz ended by throwing himself into the arms of the minister.

It was quite an event when the father and daughter re-entered the church.

The pastor thundered with more virulence than ever against the master of Escal-Vigor and his concubine. During the service Claudie contemplated with eager curiosity the frescoes representing the martyrdom of St. Olfgar.

In returning to Bomberg's bosom the Burgomaster broke for good and all with Kehlmark. Govaertz, still by the advice of Claudie, accentuated this rupture by recalling Guidon; but the latter had meanwhile attained his majority, and he accorded his father's request the same sort of welcome he had formerly dealt out to the appeal of the minister.

The youngster's cheeky insubordination certainly surprised Claudie, but did not otherwise awaken her suspicions.

As for the people at Escal-Vigor, they lived solely to themselves. Since the dismissal of Landrillon Kehlmark had ceased his visits at Les Pelerins. It was that indeed, which had determined Claudie to make war on him.

Kehlmark, again transfigured, had reconquered all his courage and philosophy. During the period of his heart-rending explanations with Blandine he had fallen again into his melancholy humours, but now he had overcome himself and broken with the last links that bound him to Christianity. He believed himself better than a rebel, he held himself an apostle; it was he now who would take the offensive and judge his judges.

While waiting for an opportunity to take the field he armed himself with reading, compiled documents, and collected in history and literature illustrious examples to be used as apologetics. The physician, once consulted by Madame de Kehlmark, certainly never suspected what kind of apostleship the young man would espouse, whose genius and exceptional destiny he had so clearly foreseen.

At what precise moment did Landrillon resolve to communicate secretly to Bomberg, and to him only, presumptive evidence against the

Count's conduct? Probably, on the day on which Claudie gave him to understand that she was still deeply attached to Kehlmark.

At the first words, which the minister heard of the passional aberration on the part of his enemy, he feigned a sort of scandalised pain and professional commiseration. At bottom, he rejoiced! But how to make use of this lucky, well-timed scandal against the Count? There were no proofs, and even had there been, it would be necessary to publish the shame of the young Govaertz. The two allies agreed to wait for a suitable occasion. Who knows, perhaps they might succeed some day in turning the youth, who had been led astray, against his execrable undoer?

Meanwhile, the Dykgrave's popularity continued to diminish. Landrillon applied himself again, with some hope of success, to work upon those Klaarvatsch vagabonds, who had so long been the Count's chosen companions, the wildest of whom still remained in his service.

"How is it I never guessed all that sooner?" reflected Bomberg striking his head, after the departure of the informer. "Treble blockhead that I am! Everything should have warned me and given me intuition of these horrors! Did not the parents of this libertine love each other to an excess that cried to heaven for vengeance? Living only for themselves, limiting the purpose of the universe to their exclusive corporal and moral duality, in their monstrous egoism they had wished even not to have children, so much had they dreaded to lose touch one of the other!"

The minister had been informed as to this particularity by his predecessor; Henry was not born except by chance, after several years of this unnatural marriage.

Moreover, at the now distant period when Henry de Kehlmark was tormenting his conscience on account of his inversion, having learned from his grandmother how excessively his parents had adored each other, he attributed his anomaly to the impious regret which his parents must have experienced at the time of his conception. Doubtless they were vexed with themselves at having brought into the world a being who would introduce himself, like an interloper, into the midst of their mutual endearments. The young Count had long imagined that he had been begotten under the governance of this maternal displeasure. This sentiment of aversion had not proved of long duration in his mother, who was a loving woman whereof Henry had had abundant proof. Nevertheless, he remained convinced up to the day of his complete moral emancipation, that the child procreated under the influence of an antipathy would be fatally unbalanced in his relations and would render unto all womankind the deep repugnance which his mother had, at a certain moment, manifested towards him.

This conviction minister Bomberg himself still tenaciously held.

But now, Henry had returned to the sentiment of his dignity, his autonomy, and his conscience. With Guidon and Blandine he felt himself strong enough to create a religion of absolute love, as well homogenic as heterogenic. He lived in a state of exaltation, like a prophet on the point of setting out on an imperative and dangerous mission.

II

In a few days Kehlmark, Blandine, and Guidon were to leave Escal-Vigor, without expectation of return. Blandine, warned by presentiment, hurried on the preparations for departure. She longed to find herself back again in the great town, and once more beneath the roof of that villa where the revered Dowager of Kehlmark had breathed her last.

Landrillon saw his prey escaping him. Whilst he was quite hopeful of winning Claudie, he was still more anxious to take his fill of revenge on the people of the château. He determined therefore, to hurry events forwards on the one side and the other.

It was the eve of the Bacchanalian fair at Smaragdis, the sacramental season for marriage engagements. Landrillon betook himself to Les Pelerins and pressed Claudie to make her choice between the Count and him. The rustic beauty asked for a few hours of respite. She intended on the following morning to make one further and final endeavour to secure the Count.

"Damn it, how is it that all the women get inflamed for this fellow?" cried Landrillon. "No, no, Claudie, you'll get no further by being obstinate on the subject. Give me a chance, now that he's ruined. I'm worth more than he is from every point of view. Come, only say the word!"

"Not before I have spoken to him for the last time."

"Bother for nothing! As well hope to warm up a frozen dead body, or to make a man of a—"

Landrillon reined himself in and did not let out the abominable word which was on his lips.

"It's only a question of knowing how to go about it," observed Claudie.

"More attractive girls than thou would lose their pains. Go on now, art really so anxious to become a Countess?"

"Yes, if you'll have it so."

"But when I tell thee there's not a farthing left; it's Blandine who keeps him now. In a few days they'll have left the country and the château will be sold off. If thou wilt, Claudie, we could marry and buy up Escal-Vigor. . ."

"No; Kehlmark shall be my husband. There must be a Countess in a chateau. Besides, he now loves no longer this Blandine."

"But he doesn't love thee anymore for that either." "But he will love me."

"Never!"

"Why do you say never?" "Thou'lt see!"

"Listen," she said to him, "thou know'st the usage that prevails in this island; tomorrow is the great day of the Annual Fair, St. Olfgar's day. Now, notwithstanding the Catholic or Protestant bishops, since the time when the women of Smaragdis tore to pieces the apostle who refused himself to their folly, at each Anniversary of the Martyrdom the young girls have the custom of declaring themselves to the timid or backward youth whom they've set eyes upon for husband. I'm going to use this right. Tomorrow morning I shall go to Escal-Vigor, and I'm pretty confident of returning from the chateau with the promise of its master."

"Stuff and nonsense!"

"Thou doesn't believe it? Well I'm so sure of it for my part that if he refuses me I'll give myself to thee, Landrillon. I will be thy wife, and even tomorrow night, after the dance is over, I'll pay thee down cash on the spot."

By this brutal promise, the proud-minded hussy did not for a minute imagine she engaged herself to anything.

"In that case, I'm going to run and get our banns published," cried Landrillon exultingly, knowing as he did, better than the vulgar, slow-witted woman, where he stood as regards the weak matrimonial inclinations of his former master.

"May St. Olfgar aid thee!" he added jeeringly, as she retired, already convinced of her approaching conquest.

The Dykgrave received Claudie with much dignity and deference. His air of serene melancholy awed his visitor at first. But all the same, she presently told him without any oratorical preliminaries, the object of her visit.

Kehlmark did not treat her with disdain; he merely interrupted her with a distant gesture and thanked her with a smile, which appeared however, to the coarse peasant girl more like defiance, a sort of mockery, incapable as she was of detecting in it an inexpressible and tragic renunciation.

"You laugh," she protested in a rage, "but consider this, Monsieur, that Count as you are, I am well worth you. The Govaertzes, established as long in Smaragdis as the Kehlmarks, are almost as noble as their lords."

Then, becoming suddenly wheedling and supplicating and ready to abandon herself to him if he had but encouraged her by the least sign of love, she resumed. "Listen, Monsieur, I love you, Yes, I love you. . . I have even fancied for a long time that you loved me," she added, raising her voice, exasperated by that serene attitude, in which she was unable to surmise a withered grief, the scar of a long incurable wound. "Once you showed me some kindness; I did not seem to be displeasing to you three years ago, when you first established yourself here. Why that playing? I, on my side, believed you, and I dreamed of becoming your wife. Strong in this affection I have refused some of the richest suitors of the country, even certain well-known men in town."

As he did not breathe a word, she decided after a silence, to strike the decisive blow.

"Listen," she went on, "it is said your affairs are no longer in a flourishing condition. With all respect, if you were willing, there would perhaps be a means. . ."

This time he turned pale, but replied in a kindly, gentle voice:

"My good girl, the Kehlmarks do not sell themselves. You will find more than one suitable husband among your own class. Still, believe me it is not at all through pride that I refuse your offer. I cannot love you, you understand? I cannot. Follow my advice; accept a good, honest fellow for husband. There is no want of them in this prosperous island. I am not at all the sort of companion that would suit you."

The more he spoke with compunction, modestly and persuasively, the more Claudie's passions began to boil. She was inclined to see nothing in him but a haughty mystifier, or a conceited coxcomb who had made fun of her.

"You said just now that a Kehlmark was not for sale!" she exclaimed, panting with spite. "Perhaps I have not bid high enough!

Mam'zelle Blandine, according to what people say, has succeeded in getting you to accept something, anyhow."

"Ah, Claudie," he said, in a heartbroken tone, which, however, did not disarm her.

"That is enough! Let's break off this conversation, my child. You are becoming bad-natured. But I am not angry with you! Adieu!"

His cold, fixed look, strangely chaste, in which was concentrated one knows not what faith, what resolution, dismissed her better than any gesture.

She went out, slamming the doors in a storm of indignation.

"Well," said Landrillon, who was on the look out for her at the entrance of the park. "What did I tell you. He does not love thee, and never will he love thee."

"But what kind of man is this? Am I not beautiful, the most beautiful of all of them? Whence comes so much coldness?"

"My goodness, that's easy enough to explain. No need to search far. . . He is—how shall I put it?—a kiddie after the style of St. Olfgar. . . No, I'm slandering the great saint."

"What dost thou mean?"

"To speak more clearly, this fine gentleman has had the bad taste to prefer thy brother to thee."

She burst out laughing in his face, in spite of her rage. What a joker he was, this Landrillon?

"There's nothing to laugh at; it's just as I tell thee."

"Thou'rt lying! Thou'rt going dotty! How can anyone utter such lying stuff!" "Better than that! Guidon pays him back in his own coin."

"Impossible!"

"Put the youngster to the proof then; it's easy enough. He has passed twenty-one years, I presume, although he hardly looks it. Thou hast just had recourse to one of the customs of the country. There is another one which may apply to thy brother. To night, is not every youth of his age obliged to go to the dance and make choice of a companion, either temporary or permanent? We may wager that the young swell will show himself as frigid in the presence of no matter what petticoat as his protector did just now before yourself."

"All right!" Claudie said, with a voice at once heavy and hissing, "Ah, the hypocrites, the infamous fellows! But woe to them!"

"Ah, my word, now thou beginn'st to see clear at last. That's lucky! Whilst pretending to be smitten on thee, the noble sir prided himself on deceiving folk as to his real amorous propensities."

Thereupon he set to and related all that he had discovered, inventing and amplifying where he could not invoke the evidence of his senses.

She choked with spite, but manifested especially much virtuous disgust.

"Listen," she said to Thibaut, "I will surrender myself to thee this very evening. It's a sworn thing. But, on condition only that thou tak'st revenge for me on all, beginning with my brother, that underhanded, rotten wretch, whom I throw over for ever."

With a clever intelligence, born of hatred, she was resolved to strike Guidon in order the better to attain Kehlmark.

"Above all, no slander!" said Landrillon.

"Be easy about that! The season is favourable to us. This fair will excuse every extravagance!" she murmured, with a frightful smile.

For the honour of the name of Govaertz, she would refrain from all revelation of what she knew of the situation of her brother with the Dykgrave. She would content herself with placing Guidon in a disagreeable and humiliating position. She would expose him to the contact of some strapping wenches, who should be heated up beforehand for the attack, by liberal potations of beer and spirits; but, as the sequel will show, she had counted too much on her cool-bloodedness and reckoned without the ardour, the dizzy madness of her vengeance.

III

In the afternoon, on that day of the year, the women of Smaragdis wander about in bands from booth to booth, from tavern to tavern, noisy, turbulent, provocative; and then tramp the high roads from early evening right into the depths of the night.

On their side, the young men also roam about in groups, arm in arm. The males make advances to the females, but the latter show themselves even more aggressive.

At the beginning of the campaign it is merely a mater of skirmishes, simple assaults with indecent words, nothing more than show off and bravado. On both sides they treat one another with insolence, challenge and warm up one another; fling out a thousand allurements. They provoke one another by word and even by libidinous gesture. Furtive squeezings, secret taps and indecent touches, subterfuges and feints; they allure and provoke demands but avoid payment of accounts.

The two camps, the two different sexes, have the air of enemies seeking to draw one another, keeping on the *qui-vive*, defending their positions. They observe, hail one another, cheapen, bargain, job. It is forbidden to lovers to accouple before evening. In the dancing booths the men frisk and spin about among themselves, and the women do the same. Cynical, uncouth, leaping: massive and wanton leapers!

If, during the day, a band of women encounter a column of men, there is a crossfire, a canonnade of enormously obscene remarks. Closer fighting becomes longer and more general; time to steal a kiss or let one be stolen, with abundance of pushing to and fro, pinching, and other preliminary familiarities. Jackets and frocks, petticoats and breeches, get rumpled and tumbled amid the wriggling and contortions of the love-hot hurly-burly that takes place.

At nightfall, after sunset, a furious flourish of trumpets, sounded from the four quarters of the island, gives the signal for the hour of serious engagements. The lovers then join their favourite girls, and, as soon as formed, the couples, whether of engaged persons or of partners for the night only, become sacred and are left undisturbed by the pursuing hordes, that continue to roll up and down the countryside in waves, swelling like the foaming sea and as noisy, favoured by the darkness.

At each collision, defections occur on the one side and the other, pairing taking place amongst the deserters. As brazen as the men, the women do not rest until they have chosen unto themselves mates. The columns grow thinner in consequence of these repeated eliminations. This goes on until all, or nearly all, the women have secured their dancing and sleeping partners for the rest of the fête. Those left to the last are, of course, the most enraged. Sometimes the humour of the young sparks takes the form of avoiding their search and obliging the maddened females to track out the desired males and give them chase. They feign to abandon the game, play at hide-and-seek, and pretend to wish to escape the amorous duties awaiting them. Then, excited by drink, dancing, contacts, twirlings and twistings, hoarse, almost foaming at the mouth, the women wander like she-wolves in rut from one street-crossing to another, or hold themselves coiled up in copses, silent, on the watch for their prey.

In the distance, mocking songs give echo to their tragic chaunts. The quarry braves and provokes them, finding pleasure in throwing off the trail and frustrating the greedy huntresses. Woe betide the laggard, the isolated male: he will pay for the rest! Woe even to the profane, or the stranger, whom they accost; he is summoned forthwith to make his choice of a female, or else to follow and serve her to whom he is adjudged by lot. Sinister stories have long filled the repertory of the ballad singers, and Olfgar was not the only victim of the lust-scenes in the woods of Smaragdis.

Henry de Kehlmark was not unaware of the violence of these traditionary festivals; and consequently, however fond he might be of bizarre amusements, he had always avoided going out on this evening of the fair. It was indeed the only public fête, the only local tradition, of which he was most careful to fight shy. The people had, up to the present, tolerated his abstention, by reason of the very excesses and enormities of the Saturnalia. So highly placed a personage could not decently identify himself with such demoniacs.

On this day respectable girls also, barricaded themselves at home, as well as young married and engaged couples, who preferred less inflammatory modes of pleasure.

Claudie's visit had left Kehlmark in a state of depression, which he had not known during these latter days. He was grieved at the hatred with which the virago regarded him. He even reproached himself with not having confessed to her the truth. But that would have been to betray Guidon, perhaps to ruin him. No, what he had been able to avow to a saint like Blandine he could not reveal to a creature so gross as Claudie. And these thoughts made him repent the more deeply the amorous comedy he had so long kept up with regard to her.

Guidon, enervated by the indisposition of his friend, who had deemed it advisable to conceal from him the step Claudie had made, expressed the intention of going out and taking a turn through the Fair, hoping that the open air would put him to rights. Henry made every attempt to detain him, to dissuade him from going out at such a juncture. But it seemed to young Govaertz that something imperiously summoned him down there, something called him to the village. Some occult snare, some maleficent fluid hemmed them both around.

"No, let me go," said he at last to Kehlmark, "we shall only add to the fever and irritation, inherent no doubt to this anniversary, by remaining here together. We should end by quarrelling, or at least by not so well understanding each other. Never before have I felt so irritable and afflicted. One would think there was a sort of moral urtica in the air. These miasmas of bestial folly spread even to our retreat. It is better to face them under the wide-open sky. Besides, as we depart tomorrow, this will be my last walk in Smaragdis, a farewell to my native isle, where it is true, I have suffered much, but only to love and enjoy the more deeply and recognise myself in thee."

Kehlmark endeavoured in vain to turn him aside from this excursion. Guidon seemed drawn out of doors by a magnetic force which mysteriously summoned him.

Without any feeling of distrust, young Govaertz lingered over long on the scene of the Fair. Sauntering with old comrades, the thought that he was about to leave them for ever lent them a new attraction. He practised archery with them, played skittles and quoits, wrestled naked to the waist with the Klaarvatsch lads, finding amusement in these friendly and even cordial embraces, and close entwinings of warm bodies. Sometimes it was he who was thrown, at other times he threw his antagonists; smiling at his own strength and supple grace, and forgetting in the heat and enjoyment of the moment the profounder joys of mind and art.

Guidon did not even think of the fact, yet so important a circumstance on that day, that he had just attained his majority and was now of an age for an obligatory amour with a girl of the country. The law and custom of Smaragdis had ceased to be present to his mind. His reverie was already sailing lightly away into the mists of the blue beyond.

IV

The fête swelled, developed, became furious. Evening drew on, an obscure September evening. Booths set up on the parade exhaled an odour of cooked mussels mingled with the smell of bladderwrack and spawn, which was abundantly produced at the breakwater. Candles were lighted on stages and stalls. A mad cacophony of drums, cymbals, rommelpots and hoarse-throated buffoonery filled the air; the dancing booths resounded with hiccuppy accordions baffled by frantic outburst from fifes. The entertainments of the evening began in the booths of the wild beast tamers, and savage roarings made an echo to the sighing of the waves and harmonised with one knows not what human surge, what fleshly trepidation, what whirlwind of lust that was passing over the countryside.

Never had the sea been so phosphorescent. The fires of St. Elme clung under an inky sky, to the masts of the yachts and flag-bedecked barques.

For one moment, at the close of day, Escal-Vigor was seen brilliantly illuminated, like an edifice of emerald; then a veil of blood hovered over it on the side that faced towards the ocean.

Waves of men on the one hand, of women on the other, met on the outskirts of the villages. The women shouted out their coarse needs; the men, ape-like, gesticulated back their strong desire.

Guidon took leave at last of his comrades, the fellows of the wretched borough of Klaarvatsch. Being hustled, he hastened his steps in order to escape from the strange hurly-burly beginning to hem him in, and to regain Escal-Vigor. The thought of his friend came back to him, full of gentle reproach, of entreaty, and nostalgia. On his way through the crowd, meaning looks alarmed the truant; they pointed him out to each other with knowing winks and ominous whispers.

As he stopped to take breath, when he was clear of the pushing crowd and just as he was about to enter the elm-grove, twice a hundred years old, which led to the entrance of the Escal-Vigor park, a band of girls crossed his path, coming out of a side alley, and, calling him by name, enclosed him in their toils.

"Look here now at this great booby wandering about all alone on the road!" "Oh, the pretty boy trying to hook it off!"

"Fie for shame! On a Fair day too!"

"By Saint Olfgar! Why the boy has got some down on his upper-lip and has never yet touched a girl! Ask his own sister!" exclaimed one of the party, who pressed upon him, using much inflammatory language with great volubility. They threatened to fumble him, they rubbed against him with significant movements of their buttocks, throwing their busts backwards; with loosened bodices and half-open mouth they resembled the corolla of a flower swooning beneath the sun.

"They are right, brotherkin," struck in Claudie, in a horribly wheedling manner, as she came to the front. "Thou hast long been a man. Fulfil thy duty as a gallant and make thy choice. What more is wanted to make thee decide. Here are ten sturdy companions who have waited for thee, the best looking in all these parts. Yet they're in no want of lovers. Hastn't thou heard them a-whinnying after them all day, throughout the countryside? But, at my recommendation, they've agreed to give thee the preference. None of them will obey any other summons until thou hast made up thy mind. And yet, I repeat, there abound this evening along the lanes sturdy and valiant cocks enough, who're panting after these dainty hens, and who'll feast finely on those whom thou may'st disdain. Come then, make up thy mind! To which one goes forth thy fancy as a new-made man? To whom the first-fruits of thy strength?"

The young man divined the sinister banter in the flattering words, the first she had addressed to him during the long months they had quarelled, and instead of replying to his sister, he hoped to wheedle the ten other females, sturdy young wenches of the type of Claudie, girls with full-fleshed throats and well-rounded rumps.

"Very sorry, my pretty girls, but I'm in a hurry; I'll be back immediately; I am waited for at the château."

"At the château!" they all cried out. "At the château. They have no need of thee there today."

"The Dykgrave will do very well without thy services. It is Fair-day to day and holiday for man and beast; for the masters as well as the servants."

"Pleasure before work!—Love before duty!"

"Besides he has enough to do with his Blandine, thy Dykgrave!" said Claudie in a tone, which revealed to Guidon the worst of the dilemma.

"When I assure you, my savoury chickens, that my presence there is indispensable; I'm already much behind time." Then he endeavoured to pass on with a hasty step.

"Tommy rot, my boy! They'll have to wait for thee a bit longer; still thou'st got to return with us to the village; thou'rt going to dance after that with all of us and then pick out one of us to take back with thee, with whom thou'lt have to act according to the fashion of the honest folk of Smaragdis. So now prove thyself a worthy Govaertz!"

But he continued to try and get himself away, whilst they ceased not to harass him, egged on by the irrepressible Claudie.

"Yes, yes, he'll have to go through it; he's going to pay his tribute like the others. To each man his duty, to each girl her due! Down with laggards! Thy master will wait well enough; an hour, more or less, won't change things much."

He struggled wildly, not without an angry impatience; but they were sturdy-built wenches and grew only the hotter over the business. The crosser he looked the harder they went for him.

"Be bold, girls; go for him you wenches! Can no-one get the great booby to dance?"

In the conflict, they scented the tight-strung maleness of the sap-filled youth, and his breathing, hurried by his exertions, rendered him still more savoury and appetising. They took liberties with him, while affecting to caress him; pressed their hands over his body, catching hold of him anyhow, anywhere, this one seizing an arm and another a leg. One girl made a girdle, and another a necklace for him, of her arms, but he still struggled on bravely, turning and twisting himself about desperately, and would certainly have escaped the outrageous hussies in the end, in spite of all their fierce efforts.

But his flight would have served Claudie's account even less than theirs. The young man's obstinate resistance enlightened her completely as to his coldness towards the sex. Landrillon had not, it was evident, invented anything. Her terrible jealousy was now transformed into virtuous contempt.

"He shall surrender. He must surrender!" she shouted. "If he will not belong to one of you, he shall be for all!"

"To the rescue, Landrillon!" she continued. For, in anticipation of an unequal struggle, in which the opposition might prove too strong for them, she had posted her accomplice in the thick-wooded copses hard by. "Come and give us a hand, Landrillon!"

It was about time: Guidon was on the point of escaping from his persecutors, leaving in their hands his vest and even a portion of his hose and breeches.

GEORGES EEKHOUD

"Stop, Joseph!" jeered Landrillon, tripping him up.

Held down by the valet, who had taken him by the throat, Guidon defended himself as best he could, fought with his fists and feet, and even tried to bite.

"A piece of string!" demanded Landrillon. "The little wretch kicks like the devil! Let's fasten up his hands and feet."

"Yes, yes!"

For want of string, the harpies tore up their neckerchiefs. Their bodices ripped open left their throats and bosoms exposed, naked to the winds, hair hanging loose, bruised all over and with blood besmeared finger-nails, in the thick atmosphere of the wild wood borderland they might have passed for maenads.

"Let me go! Help!" cried the victim. Twice he broke his bonds. Blood flowed from his wrists and ankles.

Claudie, more ferocious than the others, but cooler and better advised, uttered a cry of triumph.

"I say, how about the strap which holds up his breeches!"

"Why, of course, they can come down now, right enough," said the domestic sneeringly.

And she herself unclasped his waist-belt, with which Landrillon then tied strongly the sufferer's legs.

This time, Guidon, reduced to helplessness, lay there three parts clean naked; for the furies, not content with taking down his trousers, had torn his clothes to shreds. Then, at the instigation of Claudie, the claws of these harpies violated in turns the unhappy youth's unwilling and horror-stricken flesh.

Guidon at last fell silent. He wept; sought to straighten himself; his twistings became convulsions; he shook and trembled in spite of himself; his spasms changed to the rattle of agony and instead of youthful vigour they now drew out nothing but blood. What did it matter! The attempts recommenced. They swore to exhaust his strength, but, utterly out of breath over their shameful exertions, they now ceased their discordant outcries.

However, at the cries first uttered by the victim and his female tyrants, other villagers, male and female, had run from the cookshops and the dancing booths. Drunken and lewd-minded, as soon as they got an inkling of the affair going on, they applauded and rejoiced, finding the jest a right tasty one. They came in troops, made a circle, elbowing their way to have a better look. Couples who had gone aside, stopped their private sport to come and take part in the erotic clowning. Quite young urchins, the gutter-snipedom of Klaarvatsch, the torch-bearers at the serenades, lighted up the scene with their torches as they watched with wide agape mouth this atrocious mystery, whilst others mimicked its revolting indecency. Others still, summoned their friends like hyenas to the quarry, and, while the instruments continued their hoarse music, the laughing of this crowd mingled therewith like the outcries of unclean animals. The young males, who had been languishing for Claudie, seized now the chance to flatter her with their gross and lascivious motions, she mean while,with gesture and word, continuing to excite the maddened Corybantes. Were they going to tear him to pieces alive? Was he about to perish dissected under their nails?

Past ages had probably seen the distant ancestresses of these immolators rage thus against shipwrecked men and dance around a flaming pile of wreckage; and, in fabulous times, Saint Olfgar must have seen similar cannibal throats and eyes gloat over and mock at his agony.

Landrillon, now irrecoverably compromised, no longer observed any measure, but flying from one to another, related in his fashion the mysteries of Escal-Vigor, revealing to any who would listen to him the foul deeds of Guidon and his protector, thus thinking to enlist religion and good morals on his side; the obscene rascal became a dealer—out of justice, the crime an act of salubrity and public vindication. It sufficed for the wretch to utter a single word of accusation for the whole island to lose its self-control like drunken madmen.

Not a single one but would have given the culprit a kick in the back. But some now began to hold aloof; whilst others considered that he had not even yet had enough. "When you have finished him," Landrillon said to the females, "we'll chuck him into the sea."

"Yes, into the sea, with him, the infamous beast!"

They were about to carry him through the Fair, away over to the shore, when an unexpected diversion took place.

V

Since the departure of his friend, the Count of Kehlmark had had no rest. He found it impossible to stay for five minutes in the same place. His agitation increased as the distant Fair approached its culminating point of frenzy. He was choking like one in expectation of a storm that is slow to burst.

"What a wild tempest of pleasure," said he to Blandine, who tried maternally to soothe him and to distract him from his depression. "Never before have they carried on such pandemonium! To hear their shouts we might think they were amusing themselves by cutting one another's throats."

For years the mad cacophony, the hullabaloo of the fair, the fire-works, whistlings, organs and trumpets, had not reached him in such violent and significant gusts. This day moreover, the electric atmosphere was surcharged with thick breaths of perspiration, drunkenness, guzzling, and violent heat of desire. Would this afternoon of abhorred Saturnalia draw never to a close!

It grew much worse when the sun set, and the erotic tumult of the trumpets resounded from one headland of Smaragdis to another, adding as it were, a leaden mist to the crimson terrors of the agonising sky. Human voices, still more strident and acute, took up the furious signal of the blaring trumpets, and aggravated it enough to inflame the pitch darkness.

Kehlmark could stand it no longer. Availing himself of a moment when Blandine was attending to the preparations for supper, he threw himself out into the park. All at once, a sharp, piercing note, a cry even more heart-rending than those bugle-calls of Guidon in the elm-grove on the evening of their first meeting, rose high above the metallic riot.

Kehlmark caught the voice of his friend. "Good God! It's he they're murdering!"

Hurried forward by this frightful certainty he ran headlong into the night, in the direction of the clamorous noise and lamentations.

As he reached the boundary of the park, ready to turn into the very avenue where the outrage was being perpetrated, there was a revival of hootings and vociferations, and he heard the name of the beloved mingled with homicidal outcries.

The next instant, he rushed into the fray, his strength increased tenfold, as he pushed aside the sinister onlookers, scattering the cannibals with furious blows. With the cry of a tigress bending over her cub, he disengaged Guidon, who lay there unconscious, bruised, his clothes in rags and stained with stuprous filth; kissed him and raised him in his arms.

His stature seemed magnified.

Armed with a cane, he struck out right and left all around him, as, with his face to the scamps and furies, he slowly backed towards the park, the crowd opening out to let him pass. But Landrillon and Claudie rallied the others, who were, for the moment, cowed by this majestic intervention.

There was a redoubling of the insults; the attack was now turned with fury from young Govaertz to the Dykgrave. Nobody took his part. His most devoted partisans, the beggars of Klaarvatsch, when they heard the accusation which weighed upon him, held aloof, silent, ashamed, disheartened, and took no part in the contest.

Landrillon hurled the first stone, and the others, following his example, cast at the Dykgrave all that they found at hand. The marksmen, who had come to contend for the archery prize, aimed, without shame, at the too prodigal king of their brotherhood. One arrow hit him under the armpit, another pierced Guidon's throat, making his blood spurt out on to Henry's face. Kehlmark, unheeding his own wound, never for a moment ceased to drink in and, as it were, caress with his eyes the outraged body of his friend; but, pierced a second time near the heart, he fell to the ground with his precious burden.

As they bounded forward to finish him off, a woman in white placed herself before them and, with crossed arms, presented her breast to their blows. Her majesty and her grief were such, and especially the calm heroism and divine renunciation revealed in her visage, that all drew back; whilst Claudie pushing far away from her Landrillon, who was trying to drag her off and claiming the promised reward—threw herself, henceforth irredeemably and for ever mad, into the arms of her father, where she brake out into hysterical laughter in the very face of the sordid Bomberg.

Blandine neither spoke a word, nor shed a tear, nor uttered even a single cry. But her presence gave courage to the well-disposed; the five poor men, Kehlmark's favourites, repented of their base compliance with public feeling, and now carried on their shoulders Kehlmark and Guidon, whose bodies were entwined in one common agony. The rough men wept tears of repentance.

GEORGES EEKHOUD

Blandine walked before them to the château. To avoid carrying the wounded men upstairs they prepared a bed for them on the billiard table. The friends recovered consciousness almost simultaneously. Opening their eyes, their gaze fell on *Conradin and Frederick of Baden*. Then they looked at one another, smiled to each other, remembered the slaughter, closely embraced, and with joined hands awaited the moment of their last breath.

"And me," murmured Blandine, "wilt thou not say a word of farewell to me, Henry! Think how much I have loved thee!"

Kehlmark turned towards her.

"Ah!" he muttered, "to be able to love thee in eternity as thou deserv'st to be loved on earth, thou sublime creature!"

"But," he added, taking again the hand of Guidon, "I would wish to love thee, my Blandine, whilst ever continuing also to cherish this one, this child of delight! Yes, to remain myself, Blandine, not to change! To remain faithful unto the end to my true and legitimate nature! Had I to live again it is thus that I would love, even were I to suffer as much, or even more, than I have suffered; yes, Blandine, my sister, my only woman friend, even if I were to cause thee suffering even as I have done! And blessed be our death to all three, Blandine, for we shall only precede thee a short time out of this world. Blessed be our martyrdom, which shall redeem, enfranchise, and exalt at last all loves!"

Then, his lips joining again the lips of the boy, which were eagerly presented to him, Guidon and Henry mingled their breath in a supreme kiss.

Blandine closed the eyes of both; then stoically, at once pagan and saint, she uttered precursory prayers for the New Revelation, having no longer consciousness of aught terrestrial or temporary, save an infinite void in her heart, a void that henceforth no human image could fill up.

Would her God call her at last into his heaven?

FINIS

A Note About the Author

Georges Eekhoud (1854–1927) was a Belgian novelist. Born into a Flemish family in Antwerp, Eekhoud was orphaned at a young age. With his grandmother's financial help, he self-published two volumes of poetry before joining some of the era's prominent avant-garde movements, including *Les XX* and *La Jeune Belgique*. His career as a novelist began in 1883 with *Kees Doorik*, a gritty realist tale of the life of a young farmer-turned-murderer. His novel *Escal-Vigor* (1899) was quickly recognized as a pioneering work of fiction for its portrayal of homosexuality, earning Eeekhoud praise from such critics as Rachilde and Eugène Demolder while exposing him to a lawsuit for obscenity. Eventually acquitted, Eekhoud continued to write and publish stories, novels, and poems throughout the remainder of his life, often focusing on homosexuality and pacifism.

A Note from the Publisher

Spanning many genres, from non-fiction essays to literature classics to children's books and lyric poetry, Mint Edition books showcase the master works of our time in a modern new package. The text is freshly typeset, is clean and easy to read, and features a new note about the author in each volume. Many books also include exclusive new introductory material. Every book boasts a striking new cover, which makes it as appropriate for collecting as it is for gift giving. Mint Edition books are only printed when a reader orders them, so natural resources are not wasted. We're proud that our books are never manufactured in excess and exist only in the exact quantity they need to be read and enjoyed.

Discover more of your favorite classics with Bookfinity™.

- Track your reading with custom book lists.
- Get great book recommendations for your personalized Reader Type.
- Add reviews for your favorite books.
- AND MUCH MORE!

Visit **bookfinity.com** and take the fun Reader Type quiz to get started.

Enjoy our classic and modern companion pairings!

Printed in the USA
CPSIA information can be obtained
at www.ICGtesting.com
JSHW082354140824
68134JS00020B/2070

9 781513 295411